International Bestselling Author

T N TRAYNOR

HOPE IN
LIVERPOOL

WOMEN OF COURAGE BOOK NO 4

1

Please note that US English has been used throughout.

This is a work of fiction. Names, characters, businesses, places, events and incidents either are the products of the author's imagination or used in a fictitious manner. Any resemblance to actual persons, living or dead, or actual events is purely coincidental.

T. N. Traynor
Publishing

ASIN : B091B8LYNP

My heartfelt thanks go to Nigel who tirelessly helps to check my books over for the many errors I produce, you are the best second opinion any author could ask for, and I appreciate you very much. I also want to thank my BETA readers Isobel & Martha – your help in producing this book was invaluable, thank you.

With thanks also to Maria for her beautiful book cover.

Maria Pagtalunan mariachristinepagtalunan@gmail.com

Books by T N Traynor

WOMEN OF COURAGE SERIES ~ Christian Fiction

Grace in Mombasa
Faith in Abertillery
Charity in Cheshire
Hope in Liverpool
Brianna Trefae ~ coming in 2022!

BORN TO BE SERIES ~ YA Fantasy

Idi & the Oracle's Quest
Idi & the Talisman of Talia
Idi & the Sirocco Witch

AUTHOR PUBLISHING GUIDE

Don't Go for Broke – Go for Book Growth

For more information please visit my website.
www.tntraynor.uk

Index

T N TRAYNOR

Women of
Courage

Book Four

I believe all women live with courage in their hearts. This series is dedicated to all women who struggle and have to search for strength. Everyday women might not win wars, find cures to diseases or become princesses, they do however, live each day facing numerous battles. Problems the world throws at them and perhaps more importantly their inner feelings of 'not being enough.' This series is my tribute to the battles we all face. Take heart, be encouraged and may God walk beside you.

HOPE

Let your hopes, not your hurts, shape your future ~ By Dr. Robert H. Schuller

Dedication

This book is dedicated to my mum, Heather. This isn't her life-story, but she has helped me to make this book authentic by sharing her experience of being a young woman in Liverpool in the late 1950s and giving me tiny details such as meeting a beau at the cinema etc.

Mum, thanks for being you, and helping me be me. I love you buckets full!

At the end of the book are a few photographs of my mum, I love them and just wanted to share them with the readers.

Prologue

THE GNARLED BRANCHES OF THE YEW creaked in the early autumn breeze. He wished for the umpteenth time his bench didn't fall under the mammoth tree's shadow. His navy, double-breasted jacket was buttoned, his trilby hat pushed down, hands shoved in pockets, shoulders hunched. He really should go. His legs were stiff, his posterior complaining. Yet he remained. Eyes firmly fixed on the polished granite headstone displaying his wife's name in weathered gold lettering. It did her no justice, he thought. The inscription was simple, her name, the years measuring her too short life, and the true, but totally inadequate memorial of *Dearly Loved and Never Forgotten*.

Whether from his army days or his compulsive patterns, he was a creature of habit. Monday through Friday was a robotic repeat of absolute discipline. Switch the alarm off at six-thirty. Wash, do warm up exercises in the bathroom (a habit from his army days) dress, eat a bowl of cornflakes, and when the Times newspaper fell on the hallway floor at seven-ten precisely, he would tuck it under his arm and stride to the train station. The paper would be read on the train to Manchester, where he worked as a civil servant. He would work dutifully and diligently, and then when the wheels of industry had sucked him dry with endless red-tape and pointless bureaucracy, he would return home. Cook something plain and eat it. Wash, put on his striped pajamas, do the newspaper crossword, and then head to bed with a book.

It had been a desire to escape the aftermath of war that had first driven him to the printed word. He had taken to it slowly; his first book taking six months to complete, because he'd kept falling asleep. But then... it had been *Titus Groan*, and a labyrinthine castle, madmen locked in the dungeon and a whopping 496 pages had turned out to be an epic just a tad too fantastical for him. And then, a few months after his beloved left him, the petite librarian at the local library had fluttered her eyelashes at him and pushed *The Catcher in the Rye* into his hands. Caught up in the young New Yorker's problems, his difficulty in remaining awake dispersed, and now against his better judgment, he found putting books down at night a trifle difficult. Still, when the alarm calls at six-thirty a lack of sleep is undeniably punishing.

On Fridays the routine changed only when he stopped off at the Tail and Hound on the way home, his tipple being two pints of bitter. Saturday he laundered his clothes, which included a fresh white shirt for each day of the week. Sometimes, when the sunlight beckoned him into the garden, he would drop off his dirty clothes with Mrs. Francis, who took in washing to top up the coffers. She always did the sheets for him twice monthly, so it was far too easy to drop off his clothes as well. He thought her mangle was impressive as she seemed to dry the clothes in no time. Plus, he was rather partial to the extra starch she put on his collars. There was no getting around the fact that a woman could do these things better than him, yet… one must push forward and strive to increase one's expertise in all matters. Continuing with his duties (which quite frankly dulled his senses) he would clean the house, do a spot of gardening – weather permitting, and lastly down his steak with a satisfactory measure of whiskey.

But Sundays… oh Lord, Sundays.

This one day a week, he permitted himself the indulgence of giving in to pain and self-pity, to daydreams and regrets. But mostly he gave in to his memories and his crushing guilt.

He always sat on the back pew in church. As soon as the service was over, he would slip out the door before the ushers were even out of their seats. He wasn't one for talking these days. He liked his privacy, and went all out to safeguard his peace and quiet. People knew him as a man of few words, and well since his wife died he'd practically become a hermit. Still, there was no need to be rude, they'd whisper behind their halfhearted smiles and understanding nods.

He closed his eyes. Instantly, her alluring face was before him. The corners of his lips rose slightly as the memory bloomed. This was his favorite one. Their delayed honeymoon had been celebrated in Bournemouth.

The war finally over, he had rejoiced not in the silencing of guns, but in the curve of her waist and in the joyous sound of her laugh. They'd drunk Champagne, danced and tried their hardest to make a baby. Oh indeed, it was his favorite memory! Her soft lips, her warm embrace…

"Wind's picking up."

Sometimes seconds can stand still in time. Seconds in which, one may ponder several outcomes of one's current situation, and all swinging on the choice of words one will finally commit to utter.

"It is indeed," were the words that eventually came from his mouth, while his mind bantered around 'bugger off, leave me alone.'

"It's the anniversary next week, isn't it? The fifteenth?"

He lifted his heavy head and glanced at the intruder of his peace. The young man before him was a decent man. He knew that, besides who else would remember that next week would be the fifth anniversary of his wife leaving him?

"I hope you're not going to say something like, where does time go?"

The young man smiled, and sat himself down on the bench. "You keep it neat," he said, nodding towards the grave. "She was lucky to have you. There aren't many who come every week to remember their loved ones."

"I was the lucky one."

"Have you not thought about finding someone to share life with? I'm sure your wife, 'God bless her soul,' wouldn't want you to be alone." The young man had taken

11

off his checkered work cap and was idly twirling it in his hands. Workman's hands, rough and scarred, mud buried deep under his fingernails.

He wanted to snap 'of course not,' but in truth the loneliness of the last five years, (not in passing years you understand, but in untenable long evenings) had become unbearable. "To be honest, I've thought about putting an advertisement in the paper, *miserable old git seeks companion, affable women with no baggage may apply*."

The young man tilted his head back and roared. When he'd finished wiping the laughter tears aside with the back of him arm, he turned a little to better regard his weather-beaten friend. "Think you'll get many takers, then?"

He had to smile. "No, but then I don't honestly *want* to make the effort to be nice to anyone. I don't want to explain the emptiness in my chest or why I don't eat pickles. It's only sometimes I get to thinking, perhaps life would be more tolerable if someone *quiet* was sitting on the opposite side of the table during meal times."

"My mum always says my dad is her best friend, and what more could she ask for. I'd like that, to be married to my best friend."

"What's her name?"

"Oh, I've not met her yet."

"Really?" He examined the young man. He was a tall, muscular man with sun-kissed skin that highlighted his chestnut eyes. Brown curly locks framed his angular face. He wasn't into studying men per se, but if he had to pass a comment or two, he would say the boy was personable and

12

fine-looking, surely dapper enough to attract the fairer sex. He certainly had a heart of gold.

"Once they find out what I do for a living, they normally skedaddle swifter than a dog with a bone." The young man's right eyebrow lifted high, revealing a certain 'that's life' expression.

"My advice to you then young man is not to tell them what you do until they're asking you to come home and meet the parents. By which time, they will be so desiring of your affection they won't give two hoots what you do to bring home the bacon."

"And I would urge you, good sir, to go find that companion. Come out of your secluded safe-place long enough to let someone in, you never know you might get lucky and fall in love a second time."

Chapter I

MONEY JANGLED IN HER POCKET. Today was a grand day! Hope had been working at Vernons for six months now and her promotion, which included a percentage of bonuses, had catapulted her pay packet from £2 10s to £4 12s. She literally bounced as she walked home. Surely ma would allow her to keep a portion, and she could buy herself something for once?

As she turned the corner into their street someone called out 'yoo-hoo.' She glanced up to see who had hailed her. A man on a bike approached with a grin. Just before he reached her he opened his overcoat to reveal his nakedness! Hope had a quick look then screamed and raced the last few steps along the sidewalk and charged into their tiny two-up, two-down in Dingle.

"Ma, Ma," she screeched.

Agatha came running out of the kitchen; the quickest Hope had ever seen her move. She skidded to a halt in front of Hope. "What's wrong, what's happened?"

"A flasher showed me his thingy-ma-ding!"

"What? Where?"

"Right outside the door, he was riding by on his bike."

With apron on, wooden spoon still in hand, and rollers held down by a scarf, Agatha went charging out of the house and up the street after the scantily dressed cyclist.

"Oi, soft lad, come back here, you good for nothing flasher! Come and show me your bits-and-bobs, I'll chop them off and throw them in the stew."

The biker half turned in his seat and blew her a kiss.

"You little…" the end of the sentence was lost as she ran as fast as she could in her dainty, totally unpractical, fluffy mule slippers.

Betty joined Hope on the pavement as they watched their mother running a marathon they didn't know she had in her. Sally sat down on the sidewalk and started making mud pies.

"Guess supper will be late today," said Betty lighting up a ciggi.

"Give us a puff," said Hope reaching over.

The two of them stood sharing the smoke as they watched Agatha return at a much slower pace, her hefty bosom rising and falling like a glorious tide. Her cheeks bright red, matched the artificial color slapped expertly (without the use of a mirror I'll have you know) upon her full lips.

"Brave 'un, he was to flash one of your daughters," called Mrs. Crawley, from across the narrow cobbled street.

Agatha waved an acknowledgment at her neighbor as she approached. "You've got to take care of your own, Mrs. Crawley."

"You do indeed Mrs. Bennett, you do indeed. Your brood is lucky to have you, so they are."

Agatha Bennett was nearly six feet tall. Her lush red hair normally fell in curly waves below her shoulders. Its lushness and color were due, she told everyone, to the weekly washes in paraffin. To observe her from a distance, you would never guess that she was forty-five years old. Her curvaceous lithe body was always adorned with clothes that were considered young and hip. Despite the cover-all apron she wore today, and her hair hidden under a scarf, her glamour still shone through. Hope always thought her ma should have gone into the movies, she was that stunning.

Without asking, Agatha took the cigarette from Betty, and with it delicately perched between two fingers drew heavily upon it. Exhaling an art form, she tilted her chin upwards and emitted a steady stream of smoke with puckered lips.

Mrs. Dickens, two doors down, was vigorously brushing the sidewalk outside her door. "Probably a good job you didn't catch up with that beatnik Agatha, goodness knows what would have happened if you had."

"What's that?" asked 'no need for a telegram' Mrs. Brown, hanging out of her bedroom window.

"Nosey bovine," Agatha muttered through smiling lips. "Another flasher, Mrs. Brown," she called in a loud voice. While under her breath she hissed, "send a telegram Mrs. Brown, just in case those in Manchester didn't quite catch what you said."

"It's probably the same so-and-so who's been stealing all our underwear off the washing lines," chipped in Mrs. Dickens, pausing in her energetic sweeping, to wipe snot off young Joe's face.

"True that, Mrs. Brown, could well be. Me Davey says, if he catches the dirty thief he'll chop him up, so I do hope… for me Davey's sake that the silly bugger doesn't come back!"

"I blame the Cold War," piped in Mrs. Brown from her bedroom window. "It's sending everyone crackers."

"I can assure you the guy wasn't feeling the cold, Mrs. Brown. He fair let his coat nearly fall off as he wobbled from side-to-side on his too small bike. Got a right glimpse of his backside as the coat flapped about, and he certainly wasn't blue, although, *I* certainly turned a deep shade of green. I think the image has scared me for life!"

Agatha drew deeply on the ciggi, the red in her cheeks was paling and that 'beginning to be disinterested' haze was settling over her eyes.

Everyone laughed, and Agatha curtsied before going inside.

***

Later that night when Mrs. Brown relayed the day's excitement to her husband, she whispered behind her hand (for all the walls were paper-thin and on a clear day you could hear your neighbors' conversations four doors down)

17

and informed her husband… 'And we all know that she's seen her share of naked men and wouldn't turn a hair at the sight of his backside. Still, it was probably just as well he escaped for the blasting she was giving him was enough to make me blush. And goodness knows what she would have done with that wooden spoon if she'd caught him! I'll have to pop round to our Martha's tomorrow an' give her the details; she probably knows 'im!'

***

Hope called out to their sister Sally, who had moved to play in the rubble from the bombed houses that still filled the bottom half of their street. "Come on you little ankle-biter, let's get ready for dinner." Sally jumped up and skipped over, and the two of them went inside.

"Out back with you now and wash your hands," Hope told her. Sally ran into the tiny back yard and washed her hands in the bucket filled with rain water. Hope hung her thin cardigan on a hook by the door and went straight into the kitchen to help with dinner.

Stew, again. She peered in the pot keeping her fingers crossed behind her back, hoping there might be some sort of meat within. A quick peek displayed leeks, potatoes and dumplings. She smiled. At least they wouldn't be hungry tonight.

Hope believed that the world thought Agatha was a caring mother, and to some extent she was, well, when

18

there was money in her purse she was at least good-natured. So long as you didn't question anything.

Things weren't as bad now as they had been when Hope was younger.

She placed the lid on the pan, and went to the sink to wash up the dishes her ma had left in there during the day.

Before the war, Hope and her siblings had been in and out of orphanages. She only remembered a few things about those days, although one memory in particular pressed against her memory and refused to fade. It was the last time they had been taken away by the social workers. Agatha had once again done a disappearing act, which involved her latest beau.

Sally hadn't been born when Betty, Hope and Douglas were dragged from the house, which had been empty of parents for eight days before anyone realized. They had been carted off to an orphanage. Betty and Hope had been put in a bed together in a large dormitory, while Douglas had been pulled kicking and screaming down the hall to the boys' room.

"You leave my brother alone!" Hope had yelled, but no one had responded. Clinging to Betty during that night, Hope had wondered what terrible things they must have done to be in that awful place.

When questioned about their mother the next day, all three of them had sung her praises. She was a fantastic ma. The adults shook their head and no amount of cajoling would make the children say anything to the contrary. Agatha might be a bit too quick to dish out a backhander or a slap around the head or to pull them along by the ear, she might drink and gamble all the money away, but by God, she was their ma and they loved her so. Family was family, and that meant loyalty to a fault.

How glad Hope had been, when the government announced in 1943, that all women (no longer only single women) must go to work, except for mothers of young children. For soon after that decree, Agatha had turned up at the orphanage and taken them all home.

Friday, 4th July 1958 – 19:42

Not long after dinner there was a knock at the door. It was Phyllis from down the road, Betty's friend. Phyllis and Betty talked in whispers on the doorstep for a few moments, until Betty cried out, "What?"

What followed next brought a feeling of shame that grasped a hold on Hope, until it strangled all joy right out of her. The war might be over, but inside their house a fight was brewing that would make the Germans turn tail and run for the hills. There were no physical punches, but boy if looks could kill, ma would be dead!

"I can't believe you went back to my Sid's house! What kind of mother are you?" Betty had tried not to yell, but the words had come out in a high pitched squeal.

Agatha's response was to slap Betty across the face. Betty staggered backwards, her hand on her cheek. Sparks were flying from her eyes and Hope placed herself in the doorway between the kitchen and living room, effectively shielding access to the kitchen knives. They normally never retaliated as an unspoken agreed upon sibling rule. To fight back, or to argue your case, was to add fuel to the fire. What might last an hour would last days if you argued back. So the four of them held their tongues and harbored their feelings of injustice. But not today! Revenge is a dish best served cold and right now Betty's overwhelming resentment of her mother was boiling for all to see.

"If a man can sleep just as easily with the mother as the daughter, then he is no man at all. I did you a favor you ungrateful sow."

Hope had to agree with ma about that, maybe ma had done Betty a favor after all?

"I'll never forgive you," hissed Betty.

Hope believed her. There was something in the eyes, hardened and dark.

"You'll get over it." Agatha said somewhat unmoved, like the whole thing bored her. Well, let's face it; men must bore her because she could never find one she wanted to be with for longer than ten minutes. It was no secret that the four of them all had different fathers. Betty's father Harry had walked out one day and no one knew where he was, or whether he was even still alive, for he would have surely been enlisted. A single photograph taken on Harry and Agatha's wedding day was the only proof they had that he had ever existed, beyond his daughter Betty that is. Hope's dad had been a sailor apparently, who had promised Agatha an exciting life but after a short leave of two weeks had returned to his ship and was never seen again. Douglas's dad had been an American airman and apparently a one-night stand. Sally also arrived after a one-night stand and no one even knew his name.

"I'm going out, when I come back you had better have put your mouth in order for I won't be spoken to like that. In fact, speak to me like that one more time and you can get out and stay out!" Agatha pulled her coat off the peg and pulled it on. "Hope!"

Hope jumped. "Yes, ma?"

"Hand it over." Agatha stuck out her hand.

Hope's spirits sank. In this mood there would be no way ma would give her any more than the normal few bob pocket money. She put her hand in her pocket, drew out the little brown envelope that contained her weekly wage (boosted by the bonus), and halfheartedly offered it to her mother.

Agatha snatched it off her. "I'll give you your pocket money later," she said opening the door.

Keep quiet, keep quiet screamed in her head, as Hope put her clenched fists into her pockets.

Hope and Betty stood absolutely still listening to the clip-clop of Agatha's heels as she walked off to drink and gamble away all of Hope's wages. When it was obvious she wasn't returning, Betty broke down and started sobbing. Hope was with her in an instant; arms wrapped tightly around her and crying with sympathy and anger.

"It's a good job Douglas isn't home yet, he might have given the old queen a knuckle sandwich," said Hope, trying to cheer Betty up.

"Where is he anyway?"

"He said he thought he might have found a job, I suppose he must have got it otherwise he'd be home by now."

"Hope?" They looked up to see a distressed Sally standing on the stairs.

"Ahh, come on sweetie, it's alright," said Hope, opening up her arms for Sally to come in for a hug.

Chapter 2

MR. TARONE SMITH OPENED HIS SUITCASE. Hope peered over the shoulders of her mother and sister. Maybe, fingers crossed behind her back, ma would let her pick out something pretty for herself.

She was used to hand-me-downs; in fact it was all she had ever worn. But now she was earning and contributing to the household she believed strongly that it was her turn to have something new. Not that Mr. Smith had any off-the-peg clothes you understand, no, in fact everything in his suitcase was secondhand, things he'd picked up from various places and people. But they were all new to the Bennetts and that's all that mattered.

Hope had been to the Grafton dance hall a few times, but she'd always gone in her work pencil skirt and white blouse. She longed to wear something different, something cute and feminine. She tried crossing her toes as well as her fingers.

"What yur seh, Mrs. Bennett, got me some *fine*... dings 'ere."

Agatha was lifting up items to the light of the small window and dropping them back down again just as quick.

After a few minutes of inspection, she finally showed Mr. Smith a soft, almost see-through blouse. "How much?"

"To you Mrs. Bennett, one pound ten shillings."

Haggling began, as it always did. Ma went on until it seemed she had worn him down.

"Yur know me clobber is right fine cloth, Mrs. Bennett. Do me an injustice you do, makin' me drop so low."

"Mrs. Brown told me what she paid for clobber last week, so I know you've been overcharging us," Agatha said, standing up and putting her hands on her hips in a 'brook no nonsense' fashion.

"I'm tellin' no lies when I say, blabba mout that missus is."

The deal was made at nineteen shillings. Mr. Smith started putting the clothes back in the suitcase. Normally, Hope would help him to fold them neatly, but today she was too despondent and left them to it. She headed towards the door.

"Where you going?" Agatha called after her.

"For a walk Ma, won't be long."

"Well, if you're going out, take a few pennies out of my purse and fetch us some bones from the butchers."

"Ack, Ma, can't you send our Sally?"

"Not with all those scallies hanging around, no I can't. Stop your back-chat and get going."

Hope went into Agatha's purse and took out tuppence before heading off. She hated this task. She was acutely aware that the butcher knew they didn't have a dog. Still, when she requested the bones he was always polite and never let on. She dragged her feet as she went. Of late a doom-and-gloom cloud seemed to hover around her head and nothing she did would shift it. She surmised that as she was getting older the injustice of her life heaped on her by her self-centered mother was getting too unbearable.

Her only way out as far as she could see, would be to find a man and marry him. Her conscience tugged at her because she loved her siblings to death, and she'd practically raised Sally as her own daughter.

The bell jingled its merry tune as she entered J. B. Withercombe & Son Butchers.

She waited while he served two customers already in the shop. She tried not to fixate on the different slabs of meat on display, but her glance kept landing on the lamb chops. To her utter embarrassment her stomach growled voraciously. She was aware of heat rising up her neck and forced a smile upon her cheeks.

"So love, what can I get you?"

Mr. Withercombe was such a cordial man. He might have a portly figure, and a moustache that was way too long, but he also had kind eyes and a pleasant manner. How different their lives would be if ma would only court someone personable like him! His white jacket was pristine and even his black and white striped apron was spotless. He always wore his straw hat at an angle, and he came across just dandy.

"Some bones for the dog, please."

He tried to hide it but she saw. Pity. She cringed. Lordy, but she hated coming in asking for bones, it was akin to begging as far as she was concerned.

"Usual tuppence?"

Hope nodded.

He placed a pile of beef bones on the counter and wrapped them well in newspaper. Without any further comment he handed them over, she smiled passed him the money and was out of the door as quickly as possible.

On the way home she began to ponder on the reason for living. She couldn't understand why they all continued to live when life was so hard. Surely, it would be best if she took matters into her own hands and ended it?

After Agatha's betrayal of sleeping with Betty's fella, things in the house had been awful. Whereas they normally always found something to laugh about, now the siblings were quiet, and the silence was killing Hope. Always known for as a chatterbox, Hope also sang all the time, except for when she was at work. In the last month, she hadn't once managed to sing Doris Day's Que Sera, Sera, which was currently her favorite song. She'd sung it so much in the last year that the family had started groaning as soon as she began. *'The futures not ours to see'* oh, that line resonated with her soul. Well, there had been no singing this week either. This week had been filled with a silence that killed all hope and joy.

Douglas had got a job and was going to be a merchant seaman. The ship wasn't sailing for a month, but he'd been employed to start straight away to work on getting the ship sea worthy and shipshape. All three sisters had sobbed on him, begging him to not to go. He'd hugged them all but nothing they'd said had changed his mind. A few nights after he'd told them, Hope overhead Douglas whispering to Betty saying he'd had enough and if he stayed here he might end up doing something he regretted. She understood, and part of her was glad he was getting out. The other part of her clung to selfishness as she wanted him to stay and lighten her days, what was she going to do without his jokes and mischievous ways?

Friday, 5th September 1958

Knowing that Douglas would be gone soon put a weird atmosphere over all of them; his absence would be sorely missed by the sisters. Even Agatha had begun acting a bit differently, and Betty and Hope couldn't quite figure out what was going on, in the end they had put it down to the fact that she must secretly be going to miss Douglas too, although they knew in their hearts it was the lack of his income into the house that she would miss most of all. She had done nothing but complain about Betty's and Hope's low wages since he announced his imminent departure.

***

In her pocket today was the biggest pay packet she'd ever earned. Another bonus saw her pay soar to £6 04s. For a moment she thought about taking out something for herself before she got home, she'd sat in the park holding her little brown envelope and staring at it with longing. In the end, she'd not been able to bring herself to open it. Surely, *surely*, today ma would increase her pocket money?

As soon as Hope opened the door and saw Agatha and Betty sitting on the sofa her heart sank. It was only six-fifteen, but they were dressed to the nines and ready to go dancing. She'd be left at home to look after Sally once again. They stood as soon as she shut the door. Agatha didn't need to say anything; Hope simply presented her with her pay packet. Agatha took out a few bob and handed them to Hope.

Hope stared at Betty's hands, upon which lay brand new white-lace gloves. Flashes of anger shot across her mind. What were they, a make amends gift? Where were Hope's little presents, her nights out? When was life going to be fair?

She made some bread and lard sandwiches for her and Sally, at least there was bread in the house and they wouldn't go hungry. After washing Sally thoroughly and plaiting her hair, she popped her into bed and began to read to her. Reading was her favorite pastime. Thank heavens the library was free. Books were her escape. She took Sally to the library with her every Saturday morning. Sally would pick books for nighttime stories, and Hope would lovingly select a new book to escape into. After listening to Heidi for about thirty minutes, Sally had finally fallen asleep. Hope made her way downstairs and curled up on the sofa to continue reading Wuthering Heights, for the fifth time. Oh, Heathcliff, what a wonderfully romantic hero, if only there was a Heathcliff out there for Hope somewhere. She wouldn't mind the dramatics; in fact she rather fancied she might flourish under romantic pressure.

Friday, 5th September 1958 6pm

Hope was pleasantly surprised when Agatha informed them that she would be staying home, and that Douglas, Betty and Hope should go out and not return before one in the morning!

That meant only one thing, Agatha had a new beau and she was hopeful for some kind of relationship. Betty and Hope were instantly giddy and gay. Agatha was also in an unusually benevolent mood, and gave them both double their normal pocket money so that they could enjoy the night.

Betty was normally precious over her clothes and begrudged Hope borrowing anything, but tonight she pulled out her white full skirt and threw it at Hope. "Wear this with your sleeveless black blouse, it will suit you." Joy washed through Hope, she loved that skirt! Three ruffle petticoats underneath it lifted the full circle skirt perfectly.

She tucked the tight-fitting blouse, with its finely-pointed starched collar, into the skirt and slipped on a pair of white kitten-heel shoes. She felt amazing, and so feminine! They both put on blue eye shadow and black kohl on their inner eyelids. A layer of deep red lipstick and a tiny bit of blusher and they were ready to go. Excitement bubbled inside Hope.

What if tonight she met her future husband! 'Oh, Romeo, Romeo, wherefore art thou Romeo… or Heathcliff.'

Chapter 3

Friday, 5th September 1958 21:35

HOPE HATED THE WAITING. To her it was unfair that men got to go to the pub and drink themselves silly before turning up at the dance hall. Not fair at all, in her mind. What also irritated her beyond belief was that she was supposed to sit, all lady-like on the chairs edging the room. She hated turning anyone down, not wanting to cause them embarrassment, but blimey... why was it always the ugly or ungainly young men that approached her?

She longed to be brave enough to stroll over to someone she actually liked the look of and ask him to dance. But of course that would brand her as forth-coming and unsavory, so here she sat twiddling her thumbs and wondering why on earth she'd got so excited about coming! To make matters worse, Betty had rushed off almost as soon as they'd arrived. What she'd not told Hope until this moment, was that she'd met someone new at work and they'd hit it off instantly. They were sitting at a corner table, their kissing and caressing practically indecent. Hope was cross, more at herself for having such high hopes for a fun night out with her sister than anything else. Of course Betty would dump her as soon as a man showed interest; in that respect (although Betty would refute it terribly) she was a lot like ma.

Now what was she to do?

She found herself gazing at the fabulous red and gold walls, such decadence in a city of such poverty! Still, people needed to escape the hum-drum of work, sleep and more work, and what better way to do that than to sing and dance the night away with gaiety! The band tonight was the Quarrymen, a group of young lads that had the girls pushing for their place around the bandstand. Hope and Betty had queued for an hour and forty minutes to get in, and they had arrived super early, so she guessed the band must be popular. Hope preferred the big bands, and was a little let down that there wasn't one tonight.

She watched girls jiving together, their skirts swishing out around them, and wondered what she should do. She couldn't go home yet, and she could hardly walk the streets on her own, that would cause all sorts of trouble. Just then a ruckus erupted near the entrance, and Hope glanced upwards to watch a group of Teddy Boys come tumbling in. Great, that was all she needed, a boisterous night with them around. Their quiffs, loose drape jackets and tight-fitting drainpipe trousers did nothing for her, but what turned off her more was their reputation for being fighters and gang members. There must have been about twenty of them, cigarettes drooping from the corners of their mouths caused a fog of smoke which followed them across the dance floor.

Soon they would demand center stage – in other words, most of the dance floor. The jiving was the only part about them she liked; boy she did enjoy watching them dance.

Betty, (give her, her due) did check on Hope every so often, she even bought her a half-pint of lager-shandy, so Hope could save her own money, which she appreciated.

By ten thirty, the hall began to fill, as tipsy or outright-drunk men poured out of the pubs and into the Grafton. Hope had met a girl friend from work earlier and had happily danced quite a bit, but Sue had returned to her boyfriend now, and Hope was once more sitting on her own, Betty was nowhere to be seen.

She was wondering if she should go and sit in the park until one o'clock, when her gaze turned and met the interested stare of a man at the bar. Normally Hope was prone to blushing, something she absolutely hated, but right now – from alcohol or maybe the thrill of dancing, she didn't go red. They kept staring at each other without flinching or turning away. Hope was thinking 'who are you' when all at once he started towards her. Her stomach jumped, was he coming to talk to her?

"Hello." His voice was gruff and deep and Hope instantly liked it.

"Hello," she replied with an involuntary smile.

"Can I?" he indicated the empty chair next to her.

"Sure, it's free."

He sat down and pulled the chair closer to her so they could talk over the music.

"I'm Ted," he said, offering his hand.

"But not a Teddy," she cringed even as she spoke. It was obvious from his clothes that he wasn't a Teddy Boy, plus he'd probably heard that so many times.

"No I'm not, are you?"

She laughed. "No, most definitely not."

The band started playing 'That'll Be the Day.' "Oh, I like this song."

Ted offered her his hand again. "Care to dance then?"

Her answer was to take his hand with a grin.

They danced, and they danced. They did the jive, and then when the Quarrymen took a break and a jazz band took over, they did a simple waltz step. Hope was on cloud nine. She couldn't remember ever having such a good time. When he wrapped his arm around her and pulled her close she wanted to melt into his arms. Her heart kept jumping in her chest every time she caught him smiling at her.

Eventually, her feet could take no more and she begged to stop. He bought himself a pint and a Babycham for Hope. They stood in the corner of the room, as all the chairs had now gone. Hope held the delicate Champagne-style glass, with its gold ring and little Bambi logo, in a dainty fashion, her little finger sticking in the air. She chewed her bottom lip to stop herself from grimacing, it tasted dry and horrible and she wished she'd asked for another lager-shandy.

It was too noisy to talk, so they stood as close together as they could, shoulder to shoulder. He turned, glancing down at her. Gosh, but his deep brown eyes were mesmerizing! "I don't suppose you fancy going for a walk do you?"

Boy, did she ever! She went searching for Betty, and found her still entangled in her fella, even though it was in a different corner. She yelled by her ear that she'd meet her at the gate to Grant Gardens so they could go home together. Betty nodded and waved her off.

They walked for a while holding hands, and strolled through the park. The damp night air blowing in off the Mersey River caused Hope to shiver. Instantly, Ted whipped off his jacket and wrapped it around her shoulders.

At that moment Hope knew she had met a man, who if he fell in love with her, would always take care of her. "Thank you," she said. Standing on tip-toes she stretched up and kissed his cheek.

He blushed, and she chuckled.

They only had twenty-five minutes left before she and Betty needed to head for home. She silently cursed their sudden silence as a waste of time, but something had happened to her normally over active tongue and she couldn't think of anything to say. It was like his presence had suddenly struck her dumb.

"Would you like to sit down?" he asked.

Hope smiled in return and sat down on the park bench with some relief as her feet where killing her.

"Where do you live?"

"Do you live far?"

They'd asked the questions in the same moment and started laughing.

"You go first," Ted said.

"Where do you live?"

"Tuebrook, do you know it?"

"Not so well."

"It's a little north of Newsham Park."

"Ooh!" Hope's eyebrows had shot upwards.

"Don't be afraid, I've got nothing to do with the loony bin I promise."

"Gossip says if you walk in the park at night, you can hear the patients screaming."

"I guess if you got close to the building you might, but I've never heard that me'self."

Hope shivered. "I admire people who work in hospitals, they do an amazing job. I don't have the stomach to deal with it. I know that sounds bad, but I try to help people as much as I can. It's just I couldn't stand to see a dead body. Can you imagine?" Hope became aware that Ted had gone quiet.

"You don't work in a hospital do you?"

"No."

"But you think me terrible now."

"No, not at all. Anyway, it's my turn. Where do you live?"

Her answer was pre-planned. There was no way she was going to tell a swell bloke like Ted that she was from the slums of Dingle, where bombed houses still lay in rubble, and the poorest of the poor lived sharing their homes with bedbugs, lice and rats. "We live on Woolton Road, in Wavertree."

37

"Nice, and where do you work?"

This she could answer with honesty, for she was quite proud of her job. "At Vernons, and you?"

He smiled, but it was rather sad and didn't quite reach his eyes. Then his face lit up like he'd had a brain-wave idea. "How about you meet me for a date next Saturday, and I'll tell you then?"

"That would be fine with me."

"Do you like the cinema?"

"Do birds fly?"

He chuckled. Hope was mesmerized by his lips, full and soft looking. She'd seriously like to lean in and kiss those lips.

"Blood of the Vampire will be showing at the Forum in Lime Street. Do you fancy seeing it?"

She couldn't help the smile that made the corner of her eyes crinkle, as she recalled what ma had said about horror films. 'Men hope you will be scared, so that they can wrap their arms around you in the guise of comforting you, one of the biggest tricks in a man's repertoire,' she'd said with a loud tut.

"I'm happy to watch anything," Hope answered. "Shall we meet outside the cinema?"

"Yes, perfect. I'll be the one wearing a red carnation in my lapel."

She laughed and knocked his arm. "Don't be daft; I already know what you look like."

"But I want to be sure you don't miss me." His voice was low, husky. He reached across to her face with his right hand and gently traced the back of his hand down her cheek. She had no control of the involuntary gasp that escaped from her at the thrill of his touch. She moved her head marginally to nuzzle into his hand. He moved closer to her.

Their lips met. Soft, warm. Tentatively he kissed her, waiting for her to respond. Hope moved to close the gap between them, and in so doing pressed her lips firmly against his.

They were lost then, lost in the unexpected and inexplicable joy of finding a connection. The thrill of a promising romance sprang between them, they felt alive.

"Time to put her down I'm afraid."

They reluctantly pulled apart and glanced up to find Betty and her beau grinning at them.

They got to their feet, and Hope slipped her hand into Ted's, he squeezed her fingers softly and a rush of pleasure shot through her insides. As a reader of sweeping romances, Hope had come to the conclusion that love at first sight was simply for fairy tales, story-romances were simply for books. Yet, as they walked out of the park hand-in-hand she found herself questioning whether it was possible. Could all the internal fireworks be signs that she had met her Prince Charming? Was he thinking the same thoughts?

Introductions were made between Hope and Ted, and Betty and her new fella called Fred.

The gentlemen offered to walk them home, but the ladies confirmed that they would catch the night bus from the Pier

Head. They strolled at a leisurely pace down to the waterfront, none of them wanting to end the evening too quickly. Both couples stood near the bus stop for a few minutes of intimate kissing before the bus left. The girls sat on the back seat and waved like crazy to the two handsome men through the window.

Hope hadn't wanted to let Ted go. How was she going to get through the next week? "I think I'm in love," she sighed.

Chapter 4

Monday, 8th September 1958

HOPE WENT TO WORK ON MONDAY MORNING, full of the joys of spring. If she'd known what the coming week held in store for her she might simply have stayed in bed.

Douglas had left at the crack of dawn. Despite telling everyone to stay in bed, the three sisters had got up and hovered around taking it in turns to hug him to pieces. Tears rolled like rivers despite Douglas's attempts to keep them laughing. His duffle bag was packed and ready by the door. Agatha was a no show. Her ear-splitting snores were bringing down the rafters, an indication of the amount of alcohol she had drunk the night before. Douglas promised to send the girls post cards from every port and to bring them back souvenirs that they would love. None of the girls were interested in gifts, they would much rather he stayed at home. Eventually, he managed to prise himself out of their arms. He left with a salute followed by throwing kisses at them with his hands.

She was glad that she had Ted to occupy her thoughts, because Hope felt a massive ache of loneliness in her heart with her brother's venture onto the briny sea. A new adventure awaited him, one which would take him far, far

41

away, and for months at a time. Sally had nicknamed him Sinbad, which had tickled his fancy and caused him to chuckle.

Monday's child is fair of face, and so Hope put on a smile and threw herself into working hard.

That evening when she got home her mother was out. Sally had made herself lard and bread to put her on, but as soon as Hope walked through the door she jumped up asking what they would have for tea. Maybe sixth-sense had kicked in, for on the way home Hope had stopped at the chippy and bought a portion of chips.

"Ta-da!" she exclaimed, whipping the newspaper covered chips and a bag of scrumps (batter pieces) out of her bag. Sally grabbed them and ran to the table. She waited for Hope to wash her hands and then the two of them picked up the chips and scrumps with their fingers.

"I think scrumps are my favorite thing in the whole wide world," said Sally.

Hope was thinking that to actually have a piece of fish covered in batter might be a tad better, but she smiled and ruffled Sally's long locks. "Did Betty not come home yet?"

"No," said Sally, shoving another chip in her mouth.

"But ma was here when you got home from school?"

"Only for a minute."

"Did she tell you where she was going?" Not that she ever explained herself, but you never knew.

Sally shook her head.

That night neither Agatha nor Betty came home. It wasn't unusual except Betty usually told Hope when she was staying out.

Tuesday's child is full of grace, and Hope was late for work again. It couldn't be helped; she hated leaving Sally on her own and always walked her to school when ma wasn't around to keep half an eye on her.

"This is your absolute last warning," her supervisor snapped at her. "Your time keeping is a disgrace, and if you don't want this job Hope Bennett there are plenty of people who do!"

Hope had eaten humble pie as much as it was possible for a person to do, but it didn't seem to appease her boss.

That night Betty appeared, but nothing was seen of Agatha.

"Do you think she's alright?" Hope asked.

"Isn't she always," Betty had snapped back.

But Hope was feeling anxious, something was brewing. A foreboding had been building in her spirit since Sunday, she'd put it down to Douglas's departure, but now she wasn't sure as the sensation kept mounting. Despite Betty's nonchalant attitude, Hope decided to see if she could find ma.

She walked from pub to pub and checked all the places she knew that took bets under the counter and asked anyone she met who knew them, if they had seen Agatha. She asked all the Runners (betting go-betweens) she met, but they shook their heads. Pitying looks were all she received.

Wednesday's child is full of woe, and so was Hope. Ma had returned as they were getting dressed in the morning. From the moment she walked through the doors Hope knew a bombshell was about to explode.

"Trevor and I have decided to get married." The three girls spun around in surprise, the older two were sure she hadn't divorced Betty's father yet. Agatha waved her hands at them. "Now, now, before you get all worked up and excited you need to understand that we're only having a quiet Register Office thing. No party, no guests."

Sally instantly deflated, for one brief moment she had imagined herself as a bridesmaid in a fetching new dress.

Agatha took a deep breath, one which made her bosom heave to nearly twice its normal size. *Good grief more?* Hope thought with alarm.

"Trevor has got a new job in Sheffield, and so after the wedding we'll be moving there."

"What?" yelled both Hope and Betty at the same time.

"I can't leave my job," shouted Hope.

"There's no way I'm going," snapped Betty.

And now you can discern for yourself the depth of malice that ran through Agatha, for she actually smiled before she continued. "Well, as neither of you are invited you can both do as you please."

Betty exploded. The language that flew from her mouth came straight from the gutter. Sally started crying. Hope deflated like a marionette whose strings had been cut. She sank to her knees unable to think through all the shouting, crying and shock.

Eventually the wind left Betty, and she ran upstairs to pack a bag. Agatha went screeching after her, and then a fight ensued because everything Betty put in the bag, Agatha snatched out. For the first time in their lives Betty flew at their mother. Hope pulled Sally into her arms and the two of them sat crying as they listened to the pair upstairs screaming and crashing into the walls as they pushed at each other.

Eventually, Betty came stomping down the stairs carrying a bag with hardly anything in it. As she grabbed her coat off the hook, Hope realized that she was leaving. She jumped up in a flash and ran to her.

"Where are you going? You can't leave me here. Let me come too."

A large, angry red mark marred Betty's cheek where Agatha had slapped her. Hope reached up to touch it, Betty pulled her head back. Through clenched teeth she hissed. "That woman will never see me again."

Sally ran up and grabbed hold of Betty's leg. "Don't go Betty, please don't go." The sobbing of her little sister must have reached inside Betty's heart for her steely face softened. She dropped her bag and put one arm around each of her sisters.

"Sally you're going to be fine, ma is taking you with them. Hope…"

Hope felt sick. Bile rose up inside her acidic and bitter. Betty was going to desert her too.

"Hope, you'll be fine. Ask around at work, someone will have a room you can rent. You'll have all your wages to yourself you'll manage, you'll see."

Hope couldn't talk.

"Right," Betty took hold of Hope's shoulders and made Hope look at her. "I'm going to Fred's flat. He's already hinted that he wants us to get married, this might be a bit quick like, but I'm sure he won't turn me away. As soon as we're married and we get a council house somewhere I'll come and fetch you and you can live with us, alright?"

"Me too," pleaded Sally.

Hope's heart broke. What if they never saw Sally again? Water flooded from her eyes but she made no effort to wipe it away. Her life was over. What was the point of living if everyone you love leaves you? Once you're broken you're broken forever, right?

Agatha's stomps on the stairs were heavy, a reflection of her mood.

"I'm sorry but I've got to go, if I stay here I might kill the old bat." Betty grabbed her bag and was out of the door before Hope could even whisper goodbye.

Was that a sliver of guilt that brushed against Agatha's spirit? "If, when we get to Sheffield, we can find a house big enough maybe we could send for you. I'll write a letter to you at the Vernons and let you know."

Such empty, hollow words.

Thursday's child may have far to go, but Hope had nowhere.

Trevor came and collected Agatha and Sally in the morning. They didn't inform the landlord or the school. They didn't leave a forwarding address or any money for Hope to live on.

After they'd left with a sobbing Sally, Hope sat in the house now empty of sound. Unbearable weight crushed down upon her. She couldn't bring herself to go to work. The rent, Agatha had told her, was paid up to a week on Friday, so she had that time to find somewhere else to live. 'Plenty of time,' ma had said.

Hope went into work on Friday to be told she was sacked. She couldn't remember walking home.

Saturday, 13th September 1958 just before 12 o'clock

Saturday should have been an exciting day, but how could she go and meet Ted when her life was in pieces? She couldn't do it. She was too ashamed. How could she admit that no one wanted her? She wasn't sure if she had slept at all, but as soon as the light came through the window Hope got up. She lit the oven for a little heat, and then cleaned the whole house from top to bottom. By eleven forty-five she'd run out of energy and threw herself across the bed. The bed that she had shared with her sisters for years, ever since moving into this tiny two-up two-down damp, flea-infested hell-hole. It had always been cramped, but they'd managed. Now the emptiness and cold of the building reflected the crushing sting of bleak desolation entering her soul.

As she lay on the bed considering different ways to end her life, a memory crept upon her, of a prayer taught her by one of the staff members at one of the orphanages.

The only religion that had entered her life thus far, outside of school assembly, was the fact that Jesus and God were words used to swear by. They were placed at the end of sentences to emphasize to whoever you were speaking to, that you were wholly and completely irate. Yet this nighttime prayer seeped into her memory now, bringing with it something indescribable, something akin to comfort and hope.

> *Four corners to my bed*
> *Four angels around my head*
> *Matthew, Mark, Luke and John*
> *Bless this bed that I lie on*
> *Before I lay me down to sleep*
> *I pray the Lord my soul to keep*
> *Make me safe by night and day*
> *And bless this house, O Lord we pray*

The words ran around and around inside her mind, an endless loop of repetition, over and over until she found herself saying them out loud.

She must have dozed, because she woke with a start. She peered out of the window. It appeared to be late afternoon. She ran down the narrow staircase and into the kitchen, where she washed herself with splashes of cold water, before flying outside.

"Mrs. Dickens do you know what time it is?" Hope called, when she spotted her neighbor coming back from the shops, her wicker basket full of food.

"Why it's coming up to three, love," the woman replied with a pitying smile that was more like a frown. Oh, yes, the whole street would know. Nothing was secret when you all lived on top of each other – and the walls were paper thin.

"Thank you, Mrs. Dickens," Hope threw her a cheery wave and went running up the street. If she walked quickly, she could be at the picture house before four o'clock.

Saturday, 13th September 1958 just after six o'clock

She had arrived hot and sweaty but hadn't cared, all she'd wanted was to see Ted and tell him everything about herself.

If Ted was half the person she thought he was, he wouldn't reject her just because her mother was a nut case. She had told herself this repeatedly during the last two hours. Now, she had hardly a thought in her head. She was tired, hungry, cold and numb.

She'd received many a lewd and unseemly comment as she waited, young men suggesting if she had been stood up they'd be happy to walk her home. Although she knew they had something else in mind. She raised her chin and turned her head to ignore them, she would not lower herself by affording them the answer they deserved. She was too proud to cry, remaining upright and stiff, despite her aching feet and legs.

In the end she gave up. She set off for home, her pace slow, and her feet heavy. Why hadn't he come? Had he woken up the next day without his rosy beer-glasses on and realized he'd made a mistake? It must be something like that. What if Fred had mentioned that the sisters lived in Dingle, and so now Ted knew she was a liar? *Damn my pride.* That would be a prime reason for not wanting to see her again.

Lost in her thoughts she paid no attention to where she was going. It was only when the sound of the ferry horn blasted that she realized she'd walked down to the Pier Head instead of going home.

She stopped in the middle of the path when a woman bumped into her.

"Oh, I'm sorry my love, are you alright? I wasn't looking where I was going."

Hope gawked at the woman in surprise. "Don't worry it was my fault, I stopped walking, I apologize."

"That's alright, Miss." The woman was wearing a warm camel hair coat that almost reached the floor, but her black boots could clearly be seen. She wore a matching Juliette berry hat. *Very chic*, Hope thought. The women opened her handbag and took out a petite purse. She clicked the metal clasp closures and once open took out six shilling coins. "Here," she said, offering them to Hope.

"Pardon, I don't understand, do you need me to go to the shops for you?"

The woman's eyes were soft and kind. "No, Miss. They are for you."

"What for?" Utterly shocked, Hope temporarily lost her manners.

"For whatever it is you need. Please take them."

Hope was flabbergasted. She didn't know what to say. Why would a complete stranger want to give her money? As if reading Hope's thoughts, the woman leaned over and took hold of Hope's hands. She placed the coins in her palm and turned Hope's fingers over them so she wouldn't drop them.

"I believe you should give when you can, and accept when you can't. Now please accept this gift, for I believe in my spirit that I should give it to you."

There was a massive lump in Hope's throat, but she managed to whisper "Thank you."

"You are most welcome, may the Lord bless you." And with that she spun around on her elegant little boots and took herself off to wherever it was she was heading.

Hope opened her palm. Could it be that there was a little hope left in Liverpool after all, for there certainly were kindhearted people around? She started the hour-long trudge home. She should keep the money and use it wisely she knew that, but she also knew that she was going to go and buy herself a piece of battered fish, no chips mind, just fish.

She had only been at home a short while when there was a soft knock on the door. Instantly, her heart started pounding. Had the landlord found out already? Was he here to kick her out?

She peered behind the living room window curtain and sighed in relief. It was only Phyllis. She opened the door and Phyllis came in. Before Hope had a chance to even say hello, Phyllis grabbed hold of Hope and squeezed the life out of her.

"Me ma says, you've to come to ours if you've nowhere to go. You'll have to share the bed with me and Kitty of course, but I know you won't mind."

"You're too kind Phyllis, and tell your ma I'm ever so grateful. I hope I'll find somewhere this week, but it is reassuring to know you're here."

Phyllis stayed only a short while, confirming adamantly on her way out that Hope should take them up on their offer if need be.

Hope smiled and waved Phyllis out, but her mood was dark. *I'd rather die than admit I've no one, and nowhere to live.*

Sunday, 14th September 1958

There was nothing to do. She had no energy, and no appetite for life. A dark presence hung over her. Do broken people ever mend? Can they rise from the ashes and build new lives for themselves? Where is hope in despair? Did she bring this on herself?

She had stopped thinking, crying, talking to herself, even moving. She lay on the bed all day and drifted in and out of nightmares where over and over again she caught her teeth as they fell out of her mouth.

Chapter 5

Monday, 15th September 1958 17:45

DAYS OF DESPAIR HAD LEFT HOPE HOLLOW. It seemed there was no answer to the question… can broken people be made whole again? Like the shattered egg, the shell appears impossible to repair. Glue leaves ugly scars and even then splinters of the shell are lost, irreplaceable. Hope resembled a broken shell, she was broken, shattered, beyond repair and bereft of hope. Unloved and unwanted.

The wind flowing from the north had brought with it a sudden cold bite, a reminder that summer was over. The sun had slipped into the west and out of sight, taking the last shreds of warmth with it. Almost instantly, a fog had rolled in off the Irish Sea – like an army of misery waiting to do battle.

The Claughton Ferry's fog horn bellowed across the Mersey River with ghostly echoes.

Hope's second-hand Linton tweed swing-coat did little to prevent the tenacious swirling wind from freezing her bones, especially her stocking clad legs. Her teeth chattered. The Woolworth's ten bob knitted gloves did little to stop her fingers losing warmth as she clung with an iron grip to the ferry's railings. A doctor might have told her that the lack of food meant she had no calories to burn off, and therefore she wasn't creating heat, turning the cold September wind into something more like the icy claws that normally only came with the February snows.

She couldn't see anything, not even lights from the other ferries she knew trekked the waters, all of which would be taking workers home at the end of another long day in Liverpool. She glanced over her shoulder, back towards the cabins that housed her fellow passengers. They would think her mad for standing out here, madder still if they knew her intent.

On the way over to Birkenhead she had been surrounded by workers returning home, they had all been packed on board like sardines and there hadn't been a chance to jump. Now, on the return journey to Liverpool's Pier Head, with only a few other passengers huddled in the cabins, she was building up the courage to jump. She could do this. Then the pain would all be gone.

A blur shimmered to her right and she realized someone had joined her at the low railings at the stern of the boat. Had they seen her? Surely they must have? Yet, they made no attempt to speak to her. Now what was she going to do? She couldn't jump off in front of someone and risk them jumping in to save her.

"Flipping rhubarb sticks," she hissed to herself.

"Pardon?"

So, it was a man who had interrupted her dive to death.

"Nothing." Her right foot tapped the wet wooden deck. Her low-heeled court shoe allowed salt-filled water to seep around her toes as each tap squelched water through the hole in the sole. Why didn't he leave? It was freezing out here.

"You must be cold. You've been out here since we left Liverpool Pier Head." His voice was deep and mellow and altogether pleasant, and definitely too posh to be a scouser. His continued presence however, was an irritation that began to fire her temper. The fact that he knew she had been on the ferry crossing and was now returning sent another kind of chill down her spine. Had he stayed on the ferry to spy on her? Was he a murderer? Did he have evil thoughts?

"Listen 'ere fella, if you've got any funny thoughts in that 'ed of yours, I best tell ya, my brothers will flippin' kill ya if ya come near me." Hope had thrown full-on scouser accent, complete with heavy 'clucks' to demonstrate her claim to being a Liverpudlian through and through. If the cold wasn't going to send him back indoors, then perhaps her upbringing would offend his obviously well-educated sensitivities. She also thought saying she had more than one brother sounded safer.

"You have nothing to fear, it has been a long time since I have had any funny thoughts. I would go even further and say it has been an unprecedented amount of time since I even smiled. So you see, you are quite safe on that score."

Was he mocking her? She felt confused. His words might have been sarcastic, but his tone held a note of regret. Curiosity rose and nudged her on the shoulder; she tried flicking it away with her hand, but that old tabby was the

56

bane of her life. Her ma always said curiosity killed the cat, but she'd kill Hope herself if Hope didn't stop asking so many questions.

Not yet having ever mastered controlling her thoughts she succumbed to them with effortless ease. "What you doing out 'ere then?"

"I was waiting for you to jump."

Hope spluttered and coughed. "'Ere what?"

"In the end I figured you weren't going to do it, so I came out to usher you away, so that I could have a go."

"What?"

"If you're not going to jump, then please yourself, but I intend to."

The shadowy image of the man moved, and before Hope had a chance to think, she leapt forward and grabbed his arm.

"'Ere, mister, what you want to be doing that for?"

With both hands on the railings and one foot on the first rung the man paused and turned his head to better see her.

"I wonder what it's like."

"What?"

"Death. I wonder, don't you?"

Hope peered upwards under the man's felt trilby. It was no good, it was too dark and foggy and she couldn't see whether he jested or not. She took another step closer and linked her arm through his. Prevention is better than cure, her ma would say.

"Me ma used to say, if you hold your breath long enough under the bath water you can get a feel for the afterlife.

I've tried it, but I can't stand getting water up my nose, so I always end up coming up before I've had chance to stare the Grim Reaper in the face."

The stranger burst out laughing.

"What's so blooming funny?" Hope removed her arm and stood back. She hated it when people laughed at her. They always did, apparently she was fond of saying stupid things, things that amused everyone except herself.

"Don't you think if you jumped overboard and into all that freezing Mersey water below, that you might, just *might* now, get some water up your nose?"

"I guess I would be more worried that I wouldn't be found for days, and when someone did find me I would be so swollen up with water that I'd look like a whale." Hope shuddered. "I can't bear the thought that someone might think me fat. And how would they get the water out of me so that I'd fit in one of them small coffins? Not that my ma would pay for a coffin like, she'd probably not even come to my funeral when I think about it, so what's the point of a coffin? Best they do that sailor thing, you know, when they throw the dead overboard and let the sea claim 'em. Maybe I should write a note and leave it in my pocket so that whoever finds me knows to chuck me back in, like they do when they find jetsam?"

The stranger's shoulders were shaking.

"'Er fella, you alright?"

That only seemed to make them shake more. A funny noise fell from his lips and Hope leaned in to catch what he was saying.

"Beggin' yer pardon, sir, can you speak up?"

Then he exploded. He'd tried, he'd honest-to-God tried not to laugh. Her tale was woeful and touched his heart more than she would ever know, but dear Lord she was a talker.

The ferry's horn blew across the boat, announcing their approach to the landing stage. Hope's spirits sank to her sodden shoes. She was so useless she couldn't even jump off a flippin' ferry!

"Where are you going now?" the stranger asked.

"I dunno really." And that was the truth. Home, that pit of strife was a place to bed down no more for by Friday it would be gone.

"There is a café a short walk from here. Would you care to join me for a cup of coffee?"

"Are you paying?"

He snorted before forcing his face to be serious. "Yes."

"Alright then, seeing as you've asked so gallantly."

"I'm John," he said holding out his hand.

She took it, and his hand was firm and warm as they shook.

"I'm Hope."

"Now *that's* a lovely name."

They had entered Slater Street, and Hope couldn't help smiling when she saw they were heading towards the Jacaranda coffee shop. It was second, after the library, as being her favorite place. It had only been open a few weeks and already it was one of the 'to be seen at' places in Liverpool. The owner Allan Williams had created the perfect ambiance to host up-and-coming young bands while allowing customers to peruse albums for sale, partake of a drink at the bar or simply relax at a table and have a coffee. Since the doors had opened it had been a hive of activity and Hope loved everything about it.

The aroma of coffee was overwhelming and mouthwatering. They never had coffee at home; in fact they were lucky if they had tea. Partaking of a drink in a café had become one of Hope's little treats. She normally found a quiet corner and read, while every now and again peeking over the top of the book to glance at customers. She had been in the Jacaranda three times since it opened and she already knew it was a place she loved.

It was too early for a band to be on, but the Jukebox churned out all her favorites in a low but merry way.

The walk from the dock had been made in silence, and now as they sat at their little round table facing each other, Hope wondered what on earth they would talk about. From his accent and clean cut of his cloth, she could tell he lived in another world from her. What he must think of her paper-thin outfit she had no idea.

She cupped her freezing hands around the cup and longed to be inspired by the aura of someone like Grace

Kelly or Audrey Hepburn. They wouldn't feel awkward the way she did. They would lean back and ooze confidence and grace.

"Tell me about yourself."

Hope startled. Her eyes were wide as she searched for something to say.

"Let's start simple shall we? Where do you work?"

Not simple, oh no, not simple at all!

"No? What about home? Where do you live?"

The churning of her stomach bought waves of nausea. The tiny trace of color she had faded, leaving her face ashen.

"Well, aren't you a funny bird? One minute I can't shut you up and the next you're a mute!" He'd hoped that would jog her into speaking, but no, nothing.

She picked up her coffee and sipped it and he wondered what she was thinking. Suddenly, the urge he'd had on the boat to reach out to her, was replaced by an overwhelming urge to protect her.

"I work in Manchester."

She put her cup down and studied him. She tried not to stare too hard, but now they were in the light, and he had removed his hat, she was curiously drawn to his face. He was old, she guessed around fifty, although to be honest she was never what you might call talented at guessing people's ages. He must be at least six foot, as he towered above her. His short brown hair was intertwined with gray. Although he was clean-shaven, stubble was beginning to show and that too was peppered with white. His skin was lined, creased, lived in, but it was his eyes that kept drawing her. Gold-flecked, hazel eyes rich and warm yet emanating deep sadness, she realized he hadn't been lying when he said it had been a long time since he smiled. She wondered why.

"I have a boring job, shoving papers most of the time, but it pays well and I can't complain when there are so many who are unemployed."

"My brother got lucky; he's a merchant seaman now." A little spark of life flooded into Hope's eyes.

"That is lucky, I hear those jobs are hard to get these days."

Hope picked up her coffee and took another sip, she longed to drop another two sugar lumps into it but thought John would think badly of her so she refrained. Her stomach was growling fiercely and she was thankful for Connie Francis' Stupid Cupid that was flooding from the jukebox.

"Are you married?" Hope blurted out, clasping her hands over her ever-demanding hunger pangs.

John took a drink of coffee before answering, his face solemn. "I was." For a moment it didn't look like he would explain and Hope scrambled around her brain cells looking for something appropriate to say.

"She died unfortunately, five years ago today as it happens."

"Oh, I'm so sorry." Hope put her cup down, at a loss of what else to say.

He could see her questioning eyes, everyone always wanted to know, and this young woman was no different. "It was an accident; I don't like to talk about it."

"I'm sorry, that must have been dreadful for you."

"It was."

"I got sacked!" It was all she could think of to say. "They were unfair, I had to keep taking my sister to school and it made me late, in the end they'd simply had enough of me."

"Oh dear."

"It's alright like. I'll get another job pretty quick. In fact my previous job was as a gas pump attendant at the garage, I'm sure Joe will give me my old job back, he's a good sort like that. But as I'm spilling my guts out here, I might as well tell you the whole sorry lot!"

"Pray do." John fought to suppress a smile.

"Ma's abandoned me, took my little sister and cleared off to Sheffield. My older sister, Betty, has moved in with her new man and my brother's at sea! So, there you have it, I'm about to be kicked out of my home this week, I've no job, no money and nowhere to live. I'm a right sorry mess. You ought to feel ashamed to be sitting in here with me."

She was a picture of distress, a petite waif with anxiety pouring from every cell. She fidgeted and her gaze kept darting from one thing to the next. John was overwhelmed with a need to protect her, the way he hadn't been able to protect Charlotte.

"Tell me more," he said quietly.

With no rhyme or reason to trust him, Hope unraveled her life with hesitant words. Laying no blame, she recounted her stays in orphanages. The pain of shame weighed more heavily upon her than anything else. "I'll never forget the school kids laughing at me when I turned up to class without any shoes. I'd not thought of being barefoot as something to be ashamed of until I heard them laughing." Hope choked on her words and quickly picked up her glass to take a drink.

Lord, but he wanted to put his arms around her and comfort her. He knew his fellow men at work considered him 'no RAF Brylcreem Boy' meaning he'd lost his stiff-upper-lip attitude. But he couldn't forget how he felt when he'd read the last note Charlotte had written. It was his fault she was gone and the guilt haunted him every day.

"There's a super little restaurant around the corner. Let's go and get something to eat shall we? It will be quieter there. That's if you would care to?"

For an answer, Hope's stomach rumbled loudly just as the song playing went quiet.

"Well, I guess I heard my answer," John grinned.

She wondered why he hadn't asked her about her confessions, but that didn't stop her standing up straight away. "You paying?"

"I certainly am."

"Then I'm most definitely coming!"

John automatically offered Hope his elbow as they came out of the Jacaranda, so she slipped her arm through it. She wasn't sure what was going on, but there was a growing

64

excitement in her spirit, and she was more than happy to go with this stranger for something to eat. She was comfortable with him, and hoped he felt the same.

She got embarrassed when the waiter took her thin coat. The fog-filled air had dampened her short auburn hair which now lay limply along her cheek bones. She rarely left home without putting a splash of red on her lips, so she felt rather naked without any makeup on at all. She was self-conscious about the curious glances the other diners threw their way.

John smiled into her green eyes as they sat down at a corner table.

A different waiter approached the table, looking smart in his black trousers, waist coat and crisply starched white shirt.

"Would you care to see the wine menu, sir?" he asked John.

John shifted his gaze from the waiter to Hope. "What do you think? Would you like a glass of wine or something else?"

Hope thought she might pass out if she had alcohol. "Could I have a glass of water please?"

"Of course." John turned his gaze back to the waiter who had lost a portion of his smile. "Two glasses of water please."

"Certainly sir." The waiter gave them a menu each, tucked the wine menu under his arm and departed.

Hope's first impression of the menu was to panic when she realized it was written in French. John noticed.

"The omelets here are delicious, so are the sirloin steaks and the Hawaii steaks."

Her eyes opened wide. "What's Hawaii steaks when they're at home?"

John grinned. "A huge slab of ham with a pineapple ring on it, it's actually quite delicious."

"Oh, I'd like that!"

After the water had been delivered and John had ordered their food they sat in a comfortable silence and regarded one another.

"You seem to hold no resentment towards your mother," John remarked.

"I do a little. Whenever a wave of it comes at me I remind myself that she is who she is because of her past, and try and let go of any bad feelings."

"And what is her past?"

"She was born in Wales and lived in a lovely house; they even had a cook and a maid. Her father was a renowned doctor and her mother's parents had left them the house, so they were rather well to do."

"That seems like a long way away from the slums of Liverpool."

"My grandfather turned into a gambler. Over a matter of a few years he gambled everything away. They sold the house and moved into a rented one. Ma liked it there. She said there was a brook that ran along the bottom of the garden and she was always playing in the water with her dolls' china tea set. But then they ran out of money and moved to a tiny terraced house. By the time ma was sixteen

66

they were penniless. My grandfather walked out one day and didn't come back. Ma said the gossip was that debt collectors were after him. My grandmother didn't cope at all. She'd been raised very delicately you see, ma said she took to her bed and never left it. She died a year later."

"I guess something like that would thicken your skin."

Hope looked at John to gauge his opinion of her now he knew so much. All she saw was understanding.

"Hope, an idea has been forming in my mind from the instant you told me about your current situation."

Hope sat up a little straighter. "Oh, yes?"

"Yes. You see I've come to realize lately that I'm awfully lonely, and after considerable thought I've come to the conclusion that it would be beneficial for me to seek out a companion. Not a romantic affair you *must* understand, simply someone to talk to and share meals with. You may laugh, but this week I was planning on putting an advert in the newspaper about it."

"Why would I laugh?"

"Because it is not particularly… manly, I don't think."

"It makes sense to me. You seem to have worked out what you want, so why wouldn't you go after it?"

"I think mainly because most women are looking for more than companionship. They want love and children as well as marriage, the first two I am totally unable to offer. The last, that being marriage, I could offer but finding a woman who would accept marriage when it wasn't love-based could prove tricky, don't you think?"

He took a sip of water and scrutinized Hope, until she shifted growing uncomfortable in her seat. "I have a proposition for you, Hope."

Hope couldn't speak. Surrounding her like a wondrously weird portent was the knowledge something big was coming.

"I am in need of a companion, and you are in need of a home. Why don't we get married? I can't offer you love, but I can offer you friendship and security. You need never worry again about being homeless. I own my house and I have a moderate amount of savings, there is also my war pension that you would receive a portion of once I am gone. In return you could be a sort of house-keeper if you like, look after things, the cleaning and cooking and share some of your time with me, discussing our days and things like that. You would have your own bedroom of course, I am a practicing Christian and I can assure you there will be no nonsense going on." John ran out of steam and stopped to stare at her, wondering what she was thinking.

She was only twenty-two years old and a romantic through-and-through. She dreamed of a knight on a white horse, well of a handsome young man who rode the bus really, still, she knew she was going to say yes. She would be mad not to. He was offering her the thing she craved most in life… security. Love, romance and all that, it was fickle, here today and gone tomorrow. Ma always used to say that love flew out the window when poverty walked through the door. And she was right. What was the point of romantic attachments if you couldn't fill your belly?

"What's your surname?"

"Walker, John Walker."

"Are you asking me to marry you John Walker?"

John leaned back in his seat and smiled. "Why yes I am, Hope?"

"Bennett, Miss. Hope Bennett."

"So will you marry me, Miss. Hope Bennett?"

"Yes Mr. John Walker, I think I blooming well will!"

Chapter 6

Friday, 3rd October 1958

IT HAD BEEN A CRAZY TWO WEEKS. John wanted to get married in his church, and Hope could understand that, but she knew she would feel awkward and out of place. The banns had been read out for the last two Sundays, and tomorrow, Saturday 4th October 1958 Hope would be become Mrs. Walker! John had given Hope money to cover the rent until then, and had insisted on buying her some new clothes, including a skirt and jacket suit for the wedding.

She'd been awfully uncomfortable at first, but John had been so matter-of-fact about it all that she'd finally given in to all his suggestions. With one exception, there was no way she was wearing a big white dress, it just didn't seem right. This was a marriage of convenience, as well as John's second time around, and therefore to waste money on renting a dress for the day had been out of the question. He'd grumbled a lot when she'd first put her foot down, but in the end agreed she was being sensible, and a light-gray pencil-skirt suit with a silky-soft, mauve blouse, and new court shoes had been purchased instead from Lewis's departmental store.

They'd agreed not to invite anyone to the wedding and not to have a reception; they would simply go out for lunch instead. Two of the ushers from St Mary's Church had agreed to be their witnesses. There was also no honeymoon, which was only reasonable as there was no romance.

Despite the pragmatic reasons for getting married, Hope was still nervous. Part of her wanted her siblings around her, but Sally was out of reach living at an unknown address, Douglas was at sea and although she knew where Betty was she couldn't bring herself to contact her. After all Betty had abandoned her as well, and not once during the time since ma went had she been around to check on Hope. Although she wouldn't expect her to still be at the house, she could have at least searched for her. No, she was better off without them. This was a fresh start, a new beginning with hopefully no looking back.

John had sent a taxi to pick up Hope and her few belongings. The neighbors had poured into the street to wave her off. Phyllis having informed everyone that Hope had done alright for herself, they were mighty curious. She waved to them all out of the window as they yelled their good luck wishes. Phyllis had pushed a little blue ribbon tied into a bow into her hand before she drove off, and the simple gift had bought a lump to Hope's throat. There was no sadness in leaving the street behind. She wouldn't miss the rats that ruled the yards without fear, or the mold that covered the damp walls. But she knew without a shadow of a doubt, that she was going to miss the camaraderie of the neighbors, many of whom had knocked on in the last two weeks to offer her food and company.

The drive to the church had so filled her with nerves that she'd bitten off nearly all the nails on her right hand, something she'd not done in years. She'd forced herself to leave the left hand alone, in case John took one peek at the gnarled nails and changed his mind about marrying her.

She was also longing for a smoke, but didn't want the smell to put John off either, so now she sat on her hands and told herself to be calm; she was doing the right thing.

As they pulled up in front of St Mary's Church, she spotted John waiting for her at the entrance. She smiled. There was nothing traditional about this wedding, so waiting for her at the front of church probably didn't feel right to either of them. Besides, she had no one to walk her down the aisle so it was thoughtful and sweet of him to wait for her in the porch. A warm glow wrapped itself around her as he rushed to the taxi to get her bags. She already felt cared for, and it created a rush of euphoria that took her by surprise.

His smile, as he offered her his hand to get out of the car, was tender but also nervous. Her heart warmed to him in a way she hadn't expected.

He put her bags on the floor in the foyer and then lifted a small box that sat on the table. Opening it up, he lifted out a beautiful wrist corsage. The palest pink rose was set off with deep green leaves; a smaller version button-hole was pinned to his jacket.

"I know you said that you didn't want a bouquet, but I thought a little flower was acceptable, give me your arm."

Hope lifted her left arm, and John gently folded back the cuff of her jacket sleeve and fastened the corsage to her wrist. Tears threatened to pour and prickled behind her eyes, but she forbade them to come. Today was not a day for crying.

"Thank you, it's quite perfect."

His smile told her he was pleased with her response. "Shall we?" he said, offering her his arm.

For an answer, she slipped her arm through his.

"I'm afraid we have a few witnesses," he whispered as he opened the door, "don't mind them, they want to wish us well."

Hope was shocked to see there were about thirty people standing in the pews. John leaned down towards her ear and whispered, "Don't worry; they're not coming to lunch with us."

She grinned, she couldn't help it. She had just been shouting in her head that she didn't want to spend this memorable albeit surreal day with strangers, it was as if he knew her thoughts, well at least understood her anxieties.

The service became a blur... until she repeated the words 'I Hope Bennett, take you, John Walker, for my lawful husband, to have and to hold from this day forward, for better, for worse, for richer, for poorer, in sickness and in health, until death do us part. I will love and honor you all the days of my life.' A certain 'knowing' fell upon her, so that as she spoke the words she meant every single one. That she could replace 'love' for 'be your companion' was acceptable to her, but as for the rest... in sickness and in health etcetera, she meant every word. She would do everything she possibly could to ensure that John was happy, and help them to live a comfortable life together.

At forty-two years old, he was exactly twenty years her senior, but that didn't matter. In the few times they had met in the last two and a half weeks they had discovered they had some things in common, reading being top of the list. She couldn't believe how lucky she had been in finding a splendid man like John. Her ma would probably be having a hissy-fit, and spitting feathers right now from jealousy, if she could see them.

They shook hands with everyone as they came out of the church and John thanked them for their support. Some of the women gave Hope seriously stern glances up and down, but before Hope could get upset by any of them John would squeeze her hand and give her a tender smile and she knew that it didn't matter what anyone else thought of them.

They knew they were doing the right thing and that's all that mattered.

They'd had a pleasant lunch, relaxed and were cheerful and full of chatter. Now that the taxi was pulling up outside John's house and Hope was once again awash with all kinds of nerves. After all she didn't know this man. He could be crazy for all she knew, an axe-murderer even, although murderers probably didn't marry their victims. Lordy-Lordy how she hoped there was nothing weird about him.

"It was my parents' house," he said as they approached the front door. "I have to warn you, I haven't done anything with it since I moved in. If once you're settled in you would like to decorate at all that would be fine, I'm probably open to freshening up the place, but I've got to tell you I don't like flower prints or the color pink." He grinned at her as he put the key in the door.

The house wasn't old, built during the restructure of Liverpool in the early 1950s, clearing away the air raid destruction and making way for newer homes. It was a grand semi-detached house, and after the hovel that Hope was used to, this felt like a hotel.

"Where are your parents now?"

"Father died in the war, and mother died two years ago of emphysema."

"Oh, I'm sorry John."

"I think she was quite glad to go. She never stopped mourning my father; I think she couldn't wait to get to Heaven to be with him."

"I guess it must be comforting to have that kind of faith."

"Good Lord!"

"What's the matter?"

"With trying to work out which one of us is the craziest, I forgot completely to ask if you were religious."

"I think I can confirm that I'm the crazy one out of the two of us. But why would you need to ask, does it make a difference?"

He put her bags down on the floor by the stairs and ran his hands through his hair; he was a picture of distress.

"I guess it doesn't as we haven't embarked on a real marriage, or well what I mean is… well it is real, but not normal, I mean..."

"Shall I put the kettle on?"

He dropped his arms and smiled. "I can't think of a more splendid idea, the kitchen's straight ahead, I'll take your bags up and join you in a moment."

She listened to John's heavy foot-fall on the stairs as she made her way to the kitchen. The first thing that struck her was the awful mustard-yellow painted walls. Someone, once upon a time, must have decided it would be quaint to paint the kitchen cupboards yellow to match the walls, the paint they'd used was paler but it appeared dirty and in lots of places she could see it was peeling.

The next thing she saw was the lack of a cooker. On the side sat a two ring gas hob.

"Oh, that will never do!" She walked over to the kettle on one of the burners and took it to the sink to fill it with water. The sink was a tiny stainless steel thing set in a steel cupboard unit, which had also been painted yellow. The water that came out of the tap ran clear after a couple of moments. "Well that's one good thing at least."

"Is the place not up to your standard?"

Hope heard the amusement in John's voice and turned around to smile at him. "Let's say I'm awfully glad you've said I can modernize the place a bit. The house is not particularly old, and I'm slightly surprised by this if I'm honest." She gestured round the room and swept her hand in front of her. "If you don't mind me saying, I mean I don't want to be rude. I'm sure it was absolutely stunning when it first went in." Red was rising from Hope's neck and into her cheeks. She hadn't meant to be rude and was trying to back-pedal as quickly as possible. "I'm sure the yellow was lovely and fresh when it first was painted, only over time it's faded, well, turned mustard I guess…"

John started laughing. "Here, give me that," he said taking the kettle from her and putting it on the hob. "My mum actually insisted on bringing everything, including the sink and the hob from their old house. She was what you call thrifty, didn't like to spend money."

He used a match to light the hob, then fetched two cups out of a free-standing cupboard, also painted yellow!

"Also from the old house?" Hope asked putting a hand on a small dark oak table that looked more like it belonged in a study than in a kitchen.

"No, I have to confess that was my doing. The old one broke, so I brought this down from the main bedroom to use until I got another one, it's just I haven't got around to it yet."

The two plain wooden chairs at the table didn't match, one seemed quite expensive, the other cheap… and was also painted yellow.

Hope had a bubble of happiness in her chest, it was threatening to rise and cause her to laugh, but she didn't want to appear rude and kept trying to squash it.

"The whole house isn't yellow is it?"

John gulped.

"No!" Hope squealed, "*Really!*"

"The wallpaper in the master bedroom is yellow, and the tiles in the bathroom are too. But your room is blue, and the living room is cream."

Hope couldn't help the giggles that came out. When she'd managed to stop, she wiped her eyes and looked at John. "Your mum must have been a cheerful person," she said softly.

"She was until my father died." John put some tea-leaves in the pot and reached for the milk bottle that sat on the kitchen window ledge. Wanting to change the subject, John said, "A couple of my work colleagues have purchased a Frigidaire and they think they are fabulous, if you think we could use one I'll get it ordered, once the kitchen has had a touch-up, eh, what do you think?"

Hope understood in that moment that her new husband was a man who steered clear of emotions; she made a mental note to always respect that.

"I don't think we need a fridge, but if you're willing to buy one I'd go for a new stove."

"Do you like to cook?" There was a certain glint of hope in John's eyes that made her smile.

"Yes, actually I love to cook, I've not had a great deal of practice with different types of foods," she couldn't reveal that their diet matter had consisted mostly of bread and lard and watery stew, "But I've read a load of cookbooks at the library, and I'm sure I could follow the recipes. There's one book in particular that I would love to try out."

"And which one is that?"

"Betty Crocker's Picture Cook Book, you should see the pictures, even the ones of the cakes on the front cover would make your mouth water. There's a section in there on making bread, and I'd so love to do that."

"You know Hope, there's something I've been meaning to ask you."

"What's that?"

"When we first met you had a strong Liverpudlian accent, but it seems to have disappeared now."

Hope grinned at him. "When you live in Liverpool long enough you can put on the 'scouser' whenever you want, but actually ma is from Wales and from quite a well-to-do family, so she's always spoken awfully eloquently, she used to clip us around the ear if she heard us talking in a broad accent."

After their cup of tea, John showed Hope around the rest of the house. On the whole it was a graceful home and Hope was filled with happiness at being able to live there. Her bedroom was the size of both the bedrooms back at the old house put together, and she couldn't believe she had a huge bed to herself. It would feel odd without one of the girls knocking into her at night.

After a light supper they decided on an early night.

As they stood on the upstairs landing they had a moment of silence as they looked each other. Eventually, John broke the awkward silence. "I've put the key to your bedroom door lock on your dressing table, so you can lock yourself in and feel safe."

Hope took a step towards him, reached up and planted a kiss on his cheek. His instantly flushed. "What was that for?"

"For being my knight on a white horse and rescuing me."

Before he could respond, Hope stepped inside her room and closed the door.

John raised a hand to touch his face where she had kissed it, then stood frozen for a moment as he realized he would have to be absolutely clear about boundaries, kissing was certainly off limits and he didn't want her thinking there would ever be more to this marriage than companionship.

Chapter 7

JOHN HAD GONE TO CHURCH and the house had slipped into silence, except for the pendulum mantel clock over the fireplace. It lapped up the silence and ticked with annoying unfaltering repetition. He had asked her to go with him but she couldn't face seeing all those judgmental women again. John explained that they were kind and decent actually, and that his marriage had come as a shock to them, that was all. Hope knew that both her age and her upbringing and not the shortness of their courtship would have been foremost in their minds, but kept the thought to herself.

Opening the back door she stepped out into a neat and orderly garden. She was pleased to see that John had a large vegetable patch, she spotted the tall green leaves that showed potatoes were growing, and there was also a small row of cabbages and cauliflowers.

She took a deep breath and wrapped her arms around her middle; she couldn't believe how happy she felt. She sat down on the step and lit up a cigarette. When John had found out she smoked he'd asked her to only smoke in the garden, and she was happy to comply. She normally only had one or two a day anyway.

As she was putting out the stub, a rustle sounded to her left.

"You-hoo, hello there."

Hope turned and saw an elderly woman waving over the waist-high fence.

"Hello," answered Hope moving towards the fence.

"Are you a relative of John's?"

Hope had to smile at the lack of preamble. "No, I'm his wife actually."

The woman's face was a picture of astonishment which made Hope giggle. "We got married yesterday." As if to prove the point she held out her left arm so the neighbor could see her plain gold band.

"Well, my! I am surprised at John. I never thought he would marry again, he seemed to have been mourning Charlotte forever."

The smile slid off Hope's face.

"My dear, you must come in and tell me all about it. How did you meet? Come along, come along, I'll make us some tea." The woman made as if to return indoors but stopped mid-turn when she realized Hope hadn't answered. "Please do come and have a cuppa with a lonely old woman, I so seldom receive company and I would love a good old chit-chat. I have some fruit cake!" The last had been said with a lilt in her voice and a genuinely sweet smile.

Hope smiled. "Thank you. That would be nice."

"Just go round the front, the gate is open. Then come along to the back. I rarely unlock the front door these days; I find the door too heavy and the lock too stiff. The back door is much more accommodating to an old biddy like me! Go along, shoo-shoo, I'll go and put the kettle on."

A few moments later, Hope was sitting in the kitchen with her new neighbor.

"I'm Mrs. Evans, but please do call me Bessie."

"I'm Hope Bennett... I mean Walker." Hope giggled. "It feels so weird."

"I'm very pleased to meet you Hope. I hope we become firm friends."

Despite the massive age difference, Hope thought that she would rather like that. There was something earthy and homely about Bessie. She was much shorter than Hope, so roughly five feet tall. She was rather rotund, and it seemed her clothes only just fit her, and appeared to be rather stretched. Her gray hair was coiled into a tight bun on the back of her head, and she wore small round spectacles that perched on the end of her nose. Her egg-shell blue eyes were somewhat bloodshot and surrounded by crinkles, but they oozed gentleness and motherly understanding.

"I can't believe that John didn't invite me to your big day you know," she said pouring tea from the pot into white china cups decorated with tiny pink flowers, which were perched on matching saucers. *So posh* thought Hope, who had only ever seen matching crockery in cafés before.

"Oh, we decided we didn't want to invite anyone, and we didn't have a reception," Hope rushed to confirm.

Bessie placed the tea-cozy over the tea-pot to keep it warm, and peered at Hope over her spectacles. "Now, why on earth would two people not want to celebrate their wedding day?"

Hope wondered what she could share. They hadn't actually discussed what their story to the outside world would be, 'we're just a normal married couple' John had remarked yesterday. But that wasn't exactly true. Suddenly, a desire to unburden her thoughts with someone washed over her, and before she stopped to give it any more thought she poured out her entire life story to a nodding and understanding elderly neighbor.

"My, my," said Bessie wiping away tears from her face with the bottom of her apron.

"I'm not sure John would be too pleased if he knew I had spoken about our relationship with anyone." Sudden second-thoughts (that always came far too late) made Hope feel a tad sick.

"Don't you worry, dear," said Bessie taking hold of Hope's hand over the table. "What's told to me in secret will remain hidden," she tapped the side of her nose, "God-honest truth of the matter, so it is."

"Thank you."

"Have another slice of cake; you could do with fattening up."

Hope laughed. "No thank you, but I will take a piece home for John if you don't mind?"

"Of course you can. I often drop food off with John you know."

"Do you? That's kind of you."

"Not really. You see John is always around here doing things for me. He's been helping me out ever since he moved in. He takes care of the garden for me mostly. It's completely beyond me now and it would be like a jungle out there if it wasn't for him."

John was growing more and more into a dreamboat in Hope's eyes.

"I don't suppose you ever make bread do you?"

"Why yes, I do bake bread. Not as often as I would like as is does take such an age to prepare. But every now and again the fancy takes me. Why do you ask?"

"I'd love to learn, I don't suppose I could help the next time you make some?"

"Well now, wouldn't that be just dandy. I'd love to show you."

Her friendship with Bessie Evans would turn out to be something special, and as time passed Hope would seek her comfort and council more and more.

Monday should be wash day; she could see all her neighbors had hung out their clothes already. But for Hope today was the first day of her new life, and to start it off she needed to go shopping.

John had given her twenty-five pounds in an envelope and told her to spend it how she saw fit. He'd said he'd hoped it was enough for a month's housekeeping but if she ran out she was to let him know. The only request he had was that she should buy beef steaks for Friday's dinner, he was willing to try other things during the week, but Friday's should remain the same.

She was quickly learning that John was a man of habit, and although he said the right things, inviting her to make changes with food and the house, she could see his hesitation and reluctance and knew it wasn't easy for him to be sharing his home with a stranger.

I'm going to pamper you so darn well John Walker that you won't be able to stop yourself from falling in love with me!

She'd knew the saying 'the way to a man's heart was through his stomach' and she meant to put it to the test! She walked into town and went straight to the library and to the cookery section. She had brought a pencil and notebook with her and was determined to become a culinary genius.

***

To say the Duck á l'Orange was a disaster was a huge understatement. It was so sweet and sticky, and the duck so tough that after only three mouthfuls Hope was sobbing uncontrollably. "I'm so sorry, so sorry."

"Oh, come now, it's not that bad," said John.

She wiped her nose on her handkerchief and looked at him through red eyes. "Really?" It was possible his taste buds were all kaput!

To demonstrate John forked another piece of duck and popped it in his mouth. "Umm," he said with a false smile. Slowly, the awfulness of the food began to be too much. He chewed and chewed but couldn't force himself to swallow.

Hope burst out laughing. "Oh, for goodness' sake, do spit it out John."

He did as requested and dropped his mouthful into the bin. They sat for a moment staring at their plates.

"I'm so sorry, John, truly I am."

"It's alright. I doubt that any cook gets it right from the start. It's all about practice, just like everything else in life. Don't be disheartened."

"But the duck was *so* expensive," she whispered.

"Look Hope, I appreciate your effort, I do. Now stop being so glum. I'm sure tomorrow's dinner will be a roaring success."

"I was going to attempt a pie, but I think I'll make a stew, I can't go wrong with that."

"Sounds perfect!"

"Would you like a cheese sandwich? And Mrs. Evans has given you a piece of her homemade fruit cake, it's quite yummy."

"A sandwich would be fine, thank you. So you met old Bessie then, what did you think of her?"

"Oh, she's charming, very considerate. And she's going to teach me how to make bread."

"Now that is good news. You know I was thinking… perhaps on Friday I should cook the steaks?"

———⁓❋⁓———

The next day Hope woke to the sound of the front door closing. She jumped up and got straight out of bed. She had so much she wanted to do. First, she was going to get the stew going so it would be the most tender, flavorsome stew John had ever eaten. Then she was going to start cleaning.

The house was neat and tidy, nothing was out of place, but dirt was building up on the skirting boards and boy, could the curtains do with a wash. She wanted to get the whole house gleaming before they started painting the kitchen. John had ordered them a Belling electric cooker and she couldn't wait for it to arrive. She was sure the reason why the duck had come out so badly was that she had stewed it instead of roasting it. Never mind, you live and learn as they say. In future when she read a recipe that said 'roast' she would know you couldn't boil it.

By six o'clock she was exhausted, but happy and satisfied that it had been a productive day.

"Now that smells scrumptious," said John, taking off his hat and coat and leaving them on the coat stand in the hallway.

Hope grinned. "It's beef stew and dumplings. If you're hungry it's ready now?"

"I could eat a horse actually."

"Probably got something to do with your lack of a meal last night," Hope grinned at him.

"Before you serve up, I have a gift for you."

"You do?" Hope swung around from the electric hob to face him.

He held out a flattish object wrapped in brown paper.

"It's a book?" she said taking it from him.

He nodded.

Hope ripped off the paper and let out a squeal when she saw it was a copy of Betty Crocker's Picture Cook Book. "Oh, thank you so much." She practically jumped up and down, and then reached forward to try and kiss his cheek. John took a step backwards, and the smile slid off Hope's face.

"You're very welcome for the book, I thought it would be more handy for you to have a copy here than to keep popping into the library."

"You're ever so thoughtful, thank you."

"About kissing…"

Hope put up her hand to stop him speaking. "It's alright John, I understand, it's crossing the boundaries of companionship. It won't happen again."

She looked so crestfallen that John almost changed his mind.

"Are you happy to sit in here or would you like to eat in the dining room?" said Hope, placing the book on the dresser.

"It's warmer in here, don't you think?"

"Yes, I think it is. Sit yourself down."

After a couple of minutes of silence they began chatting, and by the end of the meal they were laughing and comfortable.

Chapter 8

THE KITCHEN LOOKED AMAZING and she loved it. They had worked on it together at the weekends when John was off, but Hope had done most of it herself. She was so proud of herself. She'd never painted in her life before and she had to admit she had a natural flair for it. They'd chosen a cornflower blue for the walls and a lighter blue for the units.

She'd put a lot of elbow grease into sanding the units down before re-painting, and even Bessie had said she thought they looked like brand-new cupboards now. Her pride and joy though was the cream colored Belling electric stove. She now had an oven to experiment with all those fabulous recipes. She also had four rings on the top instead of two, and even a hot-cupboard space above the oven and below the hob. It was the perfect place for rising dough for making bread, Bessie had told her. Bessie herself raised her bread in her airing cupboard, so Hope felt exceedingly sophisticated.

In the four and half weeks since they'd got married, John and Hope had 'settled' into each other. Hope always went to the bathroom first at bedtime, John always switched on the radio when he got home. Hope lay out on the kitchen table John's bowl for his cereal and a spoon and set the cereal box next to it ready for his breakfast, after she had washed and cleaned up after their evening meal. John always stopped off at the corner store and brought home a pint of milk on Mondays, Wednesdays and Fridays. In a remarkably short time their lives had become routine and comfortable. Hope's cooking had also improved dramatically, mainly because Bessie would hover over her shoulder and point her in the right direction. She'd soon discovered that she had a light touch, and scones and pastries always turned out delicate and crumbly, just perfect. Much to John's approval! They still laughed about the duck dish, but even though she had an oven now she'd decided that maybe it was a dish that was a wee bit too fancy for them.

Bessie was with her now, having spent the last couple of hours helping her to make her first cottage pie. They were sitting down enjoying a pot of tea and some homemade biscuits that Bessie had brought round.

"I heard John whistling as he came home last night," said Bessie before sipping her tea.

"He seems to like whistling, he does it more and more often these days."

"It's a sure sign he is happy."

"Oh, do you think so?"

"I do indeed. Whistling and singing are expressions of joy. I must say I never thought I would see him happy again after Charlotte died. You're good for him, dear."

"Did you ever meet Charlotte?"

"Yes, but I didn't know her very well. John didn't move in with his mother until after Charlotte died, so I only had the opportunity to meet her occasionally. Attractive thing she was, with a voice of an angel."

"She sang?"

"All the time. They both did. Always laughing, singing and dancing, a proper Fred and Ginger they were."

Jealousy sprung in Hope's heart. She wanted that. To laugh and sing and dance, but mostly for John to love her. It had only been seven weeks since they'd met on the ferry, but Hope knew she was hopelessly in love with him.

Bessie patted Hope on the arm. "There, there, dear. You're a sweet little thing yourself. I'm sure if you give it time, he'll come to love you. But Rome wasn't built in a day you know, you have to be patient that's all."

"Did you think she was beautiful?"

Bessie cocked her head to the side and considered lying; in the end she knew that honesty was the best policy. "Yes, she was pleasant looking. I heard John laughing several times while declaring he had expected to come home from the war to find she had been swept off her feet by some handsome young man. He said he couldn't believe his luck that she'd waited for him."

"There's no competing with a dead woman who was perfect. How am I ever going to find a way into his heart?"

"By simply being you, dear. You're delightful and you have such a big heart, honestly, any man worth his salt would be lucky to have you. Come on, chin up, you've got a good life here."

"Are you coming to the bonfire with us tonight?"

"Absolutely not, those bangers scare the life out of me!"

***

Hope was pacing the house by the time John got home from work.

"Something smells appetizing."

"Oh, don't take your coat off. Let's go out straight away."

John sighed. "Do we have to go? Isn't it really for children?"

Hope's face dropped.

John relented. "What about dinner, it smells wonderful?"

Hope brightened up. "We'll have it when we get back, it's all ready."

She looked like a child herself, John thought, how could he refuse?

"Rightee-ho then, but I don't want to be out too late."

Hope practically skipped to the hall stand and took down her coat, pulled on her hat and opened the front door.

No sooner were they on the walkway when a bunch of scruffy children, dragging a straw-filled 'Guy' on a go-cart, came running up shouting, "Penny for the guy, mister?"

"Certainly not," barked John.

"Here you go," said Hope dropping a penny into the flat cap that one of them held out.

"God bless ya, miss," shouted the eldest one, as they went running down the street.

"They'll probably put that towards a bottle of cider," moaned John.

Hope smiled up at him and linked her arm through his. "I ain't no divvy, I knows what them there scallies are up to, but it's part of the fun in it? Come on ya old geezer let's get goin' before the party's all over!"

"Ugh! I do wish you wouldn't put on the scouser like that, it's enormously unbecoming on you."

"Alright, boss," she winked at him and he couldn't help but smile. Her joy was rather infectious.

Quite a crowd had gathered around the huge bonfire in the middle of the common. People were cooking potatoes on the edges of the fire and passing them around.

John shook his head when one was passed to them. "I'm looking forward to whatever that heavenly smell was back at home."

Hope's heart nearly burst with pride. Hope refused a potato but did buy a toffee apple, she just couldn't resist. "I'll save it for later," she said when she saw John looking at her.

The fireworks were a remarkable display. The beauty and magic of them never ceased to amaze Hope; she could watch them all night. Unfortunately, the main ones only lasted ten minutes and then with disappointment came to an abrupt end.

"Can we go home now?" John asked.

Hope nodded. She would have stayed and enjoyed the atmosphere a little longer but she didn't want to make John uncomfortable.

All the way home and all the way through dinner, Hope chatted away, about the bonfire, fireworks, Bessie helping her with cooking lessons and the decorating. John was mostly silent, chipping in with an occasional 'umm' to prove he was still listening. Lord, but this woman could talk!

Later, as she came out of the bathroom wearing her new warm flannelette pajamas, she almost bumped into John, who was wearing his cotton stripy pajamas. John, most uncharacteristically, looked Hope up and down causing her to blush a deep red. Her ears burned with embarrassment, as John smiled.

"They look a tad too big for you. You look like your wearing some sort of man's suit."

"They're dreadfully comfortable though, and ever so warm."

"I'm sure they are!" There was a hint of laughter in his voice, and Hope longed to reach up and kiss him.

"Well, goodnight then," she said.

"Goodnight Hope, sleep well."

She curled her toes in frustration, oh how she wished they were more than companions. Before she could do anything daft, John had gone into the bathroom and closed the door.

After brushing her hair with a hundred strokes (to make it shine) she climbed into bed with a happy sigh.

"I love you Mr. Walker," she whispered as she drifted off to sleep.

During the night she awoke with a start. She'd been having an amazing dream. She'd been singing and dancing, and then kissing. She'd been tremendously happy and excited. The trouble was that after a while she realized the man she was kissing was Ted, and it was the shock that had woken her up.

Where had that come from? Was she craving any kind of love now? Was kindness and friendship not enough for her? She cried herself back to sleep.

The next day she was riddled with guilt over being disloyal to John in her dreams. Determined to put Ted out of her mind, she set to work on preparing the meals for the next few days. She had read an article in the Woman's Own magazine about foods that were aphrodisiacs, she planned to introduce one item into each meal and see if any of them would have any effect on John.

She was cooking asparagus with dinner tonight, they were having chocolate ice-cream tomorrow (as John still cooked steaks on Friday) and then on Saturday she was going to cook the crème de la crème – oysters! After that spread of food how could he possibly not be attracted to her?!

Saturday, 8th November 1958

"What on earth is that smell?" asked John coming into the kitchen with his face creased in displeasure.

"It's oysters."

"Oysters?"

"Yes, I thought we would try something new."

She was so earnest that John stopped the biting comment he was itching to make. She always tried so hard, and on the whole nearly everything she made was edible, albeit a few tasted burnt or sour.

"I see you've set the table in the dining room."

"Yes, I thought it would make a nice change to sit in there, do you mind?"

"I think I'll be quite delighted to be leave this smell behind," he muttered. Hope looked startled. "I'm sure it tastes better than it smells," he added hastily.

Not long after they were sitting at the table looking down on their plates of oysters.

"Have you ever had one before?" Hope asked.

"No, but I hear you don't chew, you tip them in and swallow."

Hope went pale. Maybe oysters hadn't been such a clever idea after all, they looked like giant slugs and she couldn't bring herself to touch one let alone swallow it.

John picked up one of the shells that held an oyster. He eyed it suspiciously. "You did follow the cooking instructions to the letter?"

She nodded. "I didn't think we would like them raw so I baked them in the oven."

He tilted back his head, tipped the oyster in and swallowed. He didn't understand the benefit in eating something you didn't chew, but bless her, Hope was watching with bated breath.

"Umm," he said, "quite salty, a bit like eating the sea."

Hope giggled and then had a go at eating one herself. She popped one in her mouth and then froze. John could tell the oyster was sitting on her tongue. She gagged.

"Swallow it girl."

Hope went green and then ran from the room. John tilted backwards and laughed his head off. When Hope returned she carried a loaf of bread and a chunk of cheese on a tray with her, which set him off chuckling all the more.

John managed to swallow another one before he realized that was all he could stomach. "Willing to share?" he smiled at her.

As Hope sliced bread and cheese for John she kept glancing at him from under her fringe. He was decidedly charming and handsome as far as she was concerned. He was kind and considerate, a little stiff and formal sometimes, but besides that she idolized him. She'd even

100

prayed to a God she didn't believe in, to ask if He might bend John's affection towards her. No answer on that one yet, but she was hopeful. She had even made a bargain, saying that if John would fall in love with her then she would become a Christian and give her life to God. She had no idea if that was acceptable or not but she had her fingers crossed.

A strange noise broke into Hope's early morning dream, waking her up. She lay there for a moment trying to work out what she could hear. After a moment, it dawned on her that it was moaning she could hear. She jumped out of bed and ran out of the room. She listened for a moment and realized the noise was coming from the bathroom.

She knocked on the door. "John, are you alright?"

A guttural groan came from the other side of the door.

She hammered on the door. "John, John, are you alright? Can I come in?"

Then she heard him being sick. The sound of retches that come when there is nothing left but bile flooded the house. She took a deep breath and broke the boundaries of their agreement, and entered the bathroom. John was draped over the toilet like a rag-doll. She dropped to her knees beside him.

"John, shall I fetch the doctor?"

He shook his head.

"Would you like a glass of water?"

He nodded.

Hope went charging down the stairs and into the kitchen in a panic. John looked awful, white as a ghost with large black rings under his eyes. He looked really sick to her. She ran up the stairs two at a time, and went back to John's side.

"Here you are."

"Thanks." He took a couple of tiny sips and then shuffled backwards to lean against the bathroom wall. "I think you've poisoned me."

"What?" Hope screeched. "No I haven't, I'd never do anything to harm you."

"Not intentionally," there was the tiniest of smiles at the corner of his lips.

"I'm fetching Bessie." Before he could protest, Hope had dashed off again. It took only a few minutes as Bessie always rose before the sun, and was up, washed and dressed ready for the day when Hope hammered on her back door.

"Go and fetch the doctor, Hope," Bessie said, after she had placed her hand on John's forehead. "He's burning up something awful, be sure and tell the doctor that."

Not wanting to waste any time, Hope didn't bother getting dressed. Instead she pulled on her long coat, slipped her shoes on and went running down the street. Luckily, the doctor's surgery was only three streets away. She charged through the door and ran to the receptionist.

"I need a doctor, its John; I think I've nearly killed him! Please, you've got to get the doctor to him quick. He can't die, I love him. He doesn't know that yet. But I do, I love him. He can't die. Please…"

"Shh," said the receptionist, coming around the counter. "You're lucky, Doctor Hughes has just arrived. Wait here, I'll go and fetch him."

With black bag in hand, the elderly, wiry, bent doctor, did his best to keep pace with Hope. She had to keep stopping, demanding he hurry and he was quite out of breath by the time they arrived home.

Bessie had managed to get John back into bed, and had placed a bucket next to him in case he was sick again. She had a cold, damp cloth on his head to try and cool him, but John was shivering and wanted the covers over him.

When Hope saw how weak John looked lying back against the pillows she burst into tears.

"Now, now," said Bessie, "that won't do. Come on let's go downstairs while doc takes a look at John, come along now."

Hope allowed herself to be led downstairs and into the kitchen, where Bessie went straight for the kettle.

A short time later the doctor made his way down the stairs. Both ladies rushed to greet him in the hallway.

"Is he going to be alright?" Hope said her hands clasped together under her chin.

"He will, but it will take a few days for him to recover. He needs three days of bed rest and plenty of fluids. Nothing to eat today, and maybe something very light like chicken soup tomorrow, although if he can be persuaded to go another day without your delectable cooking, it would probably be best if he didn't eat for forty-eight hours."

Hope looked at the doctor in shock; there had been a chuckle in that statement, she was sure of it.

"We'll take good care of him doctor, thank you so much for coming," said Bessie opening the door for him.

The doctor started to leave but turned around on the step and looked back in at them. "Plenty of fluids, do you hear?"

"Yes doctor," they both replied.

As soon as the door closed, Hope went charging up the stairs. Bessie sighed and went into the kitchen to make a pot of tea.

"Are you alright?" Hope whispered.

He turned his head to look at her. "No, not in any way."

Hope burst into tears. "It was the oysters wasn't it? Oh, I'm so sorry John, really I am. I'll never cook them again. I'm so sorry."

"Hope, I have enough to contend with right now without your sniffles as well."

"Oh, sorry, I'm sorry."

John sighed. "Please stop saying you're sorry."

"Sorry."

John raised his eyebrow at her.

Like a dog with its tail between its legs, Hope turned to leave. As she did so, her gaze fell upon the photographs that John had in frames on his bedside unit. One was of him with Charlotte on their wedding day, and the other was of Charlotte on her own. The image burned into Hope's spirits and she fled the room before she broke down in front of John.

John was as weak as a new born kitten for days. He didn't manage to get into work all week as his recovery was slower than expected. During this time there seemed to be nothing that Hope could do to make it better. He had turned into a miserable grump, and Hope was beside herself, and went to visit Bessie for some tender loving care.

"You have to leave him be," said Bessie as she kneaded the dough to make some bread. "Here, wash your hands and take over for me. My arthritis is killing me, I need to sit down."

"Sure you trust me to touch it?" asked Hope. "If John knows I helped you make it he won't eat it."

"Now stop being churlish. You nearly killed the poor man, what do you expect? He's bound to be slightly tetchy with you."

Hope found kneading the dough to be relaxing, and despite the vigorous actions required to knead it well, she found herself relaxing.

"Why on earth did you cook oysters anyway?"

Hope told her about the article she had read in the magazine and Bessie burst out laughing. She roared. Her whole body shaking uncontrollably as tears spilled down her cheeks.

"Oh Lord, oh Lord," she chuckled.

"Well, what would you do to make a man fall in love with you?" asked Hope.

Bessie wiped her tears away. "Good Lord, I can't remember the last time I laughed like that. I do love you, you funny little thing."

"Well, no offense, but I wish it was John who loved me"

"The youth these days have absolutely no patience."

Chapter 9

CHRISTMAS WAS FAST APPROACHING and persuading John that despite having no children they still needed a tree had been quite a task. He'd struck a bargain with her eventually, in exchange for John joining in (and trying to be cheerful) with the Christmas preparations, Hope was to come to church for four Sundays services in a row (and try to enjoy them). It was fair to say they were both being pushed out of their comfort zones. John hadn't celebrated Christmas since Charlotte had died, and Hope had never been to church in her life, except for one school trip.

The arrival of a brand new 17-inch Murphy television had been a delightful surprise. John grinned as he watched Hope jumping up and down in the living room.

"Where shall we put it?" Hope asked, excitement pouring from her.

"We should put it in the corner over there," John pointed. "We'll have to move the seating a touch, but it should all fit in excellently."

Hope didn't waste time and started moving the furniture around. "Help me move the carpet, John," she said after she'd put the coffee table in the hallway.

"You know this flooring is a death-trap waiting to happen, you put so much polish on the damn boards."

"Sorry!" Hope snapped. "Pardon me your nibs, for trying to keep *your* home spic and span for you!"

"*Our* home, Hope."

The emphasis on 'our' melted Hope's heart, and once again she forgave him for his snappy ways.

With the carpet pulled in front of the gas fireplace they were able to shift the chairs around. John picked up the television, putting it gently on its side so that he could screw the four wooden legs in. When he finished he turned it upright and stood it in the corner.

"I can't believe you spent ninety-two pounds on a television," the words came out of Hope with awe. "Why didn't you rent one like everyone else?"

"Well, it does have a built-in radio as well; I thought that might be handy. And I don't do hire-purchase Hope, you should know that by now. I believe in saving up and buying something when you can afford it."

"Guess you take after your mum in that respect."

"I guess I must."

"Turn it on John, let's see what's on."

John obliged. With only two black and white channels he wasn't expecting an awful lot of entertainment. He moved around the aerial until the zigzag lines faded and the picture became clear.

"That's it, just there, you've got it clear now. Look John, it's Watch with Mother!" Hope sank onto her knees in front of the television. Fifteen minutes later the puppets were declaring it was time to go home. Hope was still on her knees and John was still standing in the same place when the narrator sang goodbye.

Hope swiveled round to grin at John.

"Humph! Extremely educational I'm sure, for *children*!"

Hope giggled.

Saturday, 13th December 1958

Her 'grump' was carrying the fir tree under his arm and muttering about the waste of money these Christmas trappings were, but Hope's heart was soaring.

After sending so many letters to the shipping company she'd finally received one back from Douglas. He would be back in Liverpool in January and had promised to come and meet her new husband. A week ago she had decided to visit Betty and invite her over for Christmas dinner, but there were new people in the flat and they had no idea of Betty's new address, although they mentioned that Betty and Fred had talked about Swansea, so Hope guessed they had moved to Wales without so much as a cheerio.

Still, Douglas was coming home and that was great. What had been even more wonderful was the delightful Father Christmas cabin that had been built in the square, she'd longed to go in and have her picture taken with the red-dressed impostor but one look at John's face when she mentioned it was enough for her to walk past. Still, he had purchased a lush six-foot tree and was carrying it home, all be it with moans about pricking pine needles!

Space for the tree had been made ready next to the television, and John placed the trunk in the sand-filled bucket that was waiting to hold it. Hope watched as John cut the strings that held the branches together, and was grinning from ear-to-ear as the branches sprang open.

"Will you help me decorate it, John?"

"No." He left her to it and went into the kitchen to make them drinks.

Last week Hope had used some of the money she'd been saving from the house-keeping to buy an album. She went over to the unit that housed the HMV record player, and popped Johnny Mathis' Merry Christmas album on, and then gently placed the needed on the edge.

As soon as *sleigh bells ring* came out of the speaker she heard John groan, and she giggled. She would convert him towards the Christmas trimmings by the time she was finished with him. "Are you listening, in the lane, snow is glistening…" Hope joined in with the song, which made John groan even louder.

By the time *chestnuts roasting on an open fire* came on Hope had the lights on the tree.

John came in. "Cup of tea?" he offered her a cup, which she took with a smile. Instead of leaving her again, he sat down in his chair and picked up his book. As she put candy canes, red bows and crackers on the tree John kept watching her, but quickly glanced back down at his book whenever she turned around. "I love this song," he said when Jonny started singing *What Child Is This*.

"It's very pretty," said Hope standing back to admire the tree.

"Yes, you've done a first-rate job there."

"Oh, I meant the song, but thank you."

They sat in comfortable silence and listened to the rest of the album. When *It Came upon the Midnight Clear* came on, Hope got up and put her hand out towards John. "Dance with me?"

"I don't think so."

Her face was a picture of disappointment and he succumbed and stood up. "Just one," he said standing up. He placed his right arm around her waist and took hold of her right hand in his left. They took a few steps and then he stopped. "This'll never do," he said letting her go.

She felt crushed as he turned and walked away. But he didn't leave the room, instead he went to the record player and lifted up the stylus and put the record back in its sleeve. He bent down to go through his record selection until he found the one he wanted. He put side two of *Ella Fitzgerald sings the Cole Porter Songs* on the table, picked up the stylus and dropped it on track eleven. When he turned around Hope was watching him. As Ella started to sing, John moved back over to Hope and once more took her in his arms.

"Now this is more like it," he said as Ella sang. *When you're near there's such an air of spring about it...* John slowly moved them around the floor; naturally he drew

111

Hope close to his chest. Her heart was beating fast; John had never put his arms around her before. Maybe she was beginning to break down his resistance? Towards the end of the song John had slowed so much they were hardly moving. At the end of it she tilted back her head to look up at him. He looked down at her, his eyes misty and sorrowful. He let her go and went to take Ella off the turntable and put Hope's Christmas one back on. Without a word he left her and went upstairs.

Hope sat on the chair, her vision blurred as tears filled her eyes. She knew that he was now sitting on his bed looking at the pictures of his beautiful, but very dead, wife, the woman he really wanted to dance with.

Friday, 19th December 1958, 21:45

Looking at herself in the mirror, Hope didn't know if she wanted to giggle or be sick. She had never owned anything like this in her life, and she blamed Bessie for the fact that she owned one now! It was freezing up here – there was even ice on the outside of her bedroom window. What she was doing in this skimpy, cotton, tiny-blue flower covered white baby-doll nightie she had no idea! Well, that wasn't exactly true of course. She was actually standing near the bedroom door so that when she heard John coming up the stairs she could pop out and ambush him in her new sexy attire! *'If John was a man, and surely he was,'* Bessie had said, *'he wouldn't be able to resist her.'*

When they'd gone shopping together, this had seemed like such a marvelous idea. Now however, as she stood with goose-bumps covering her legs and arms, she wasn't too sure. He'd probably think she'd gone nutty and ask her where her warm flannelette had gone. "Nothing ventured, nothing gained," she whispered to her reflection. She pinched her cheeks to make them rosy as soon as she heard John close the living room door.

She timed it just right and as soon as his foot hit the landing she rushed out of her room. She stopped half-way to the bathroom. "Oh John, you startled me, I didn't notice you there." She smiled, in what she hoped was her most seductive and glamorous pose.

John look horrified. *What on earth's wrong with her face?* He wondered.

"Aren't you cold?" he asked, keeping his eyes firmly fixed on her hairline. The one glance at her graceful long legs had already got his blood pumping.

"Why no," she answered, putting her hand on her hip and bending slightly to the side, the way she had seen models pose.

My God, she looks like a crocked horse, John thought, *what on earth is she doing?*

Hope knew instantly it wasn't working. Too embarrassed to say anything else she rushed into the bathroom and slammed the door shut.

"Women!" said John under his breath, "crackers the lot of them."

Hope put down the toilet seat lid and sat on the top of it and started to cry. *Cost me four blooming pounds this did, what a waste of money.* She grabbed a pile of tissue and gave her nose a vigorous blow, then when she was sure John was in his room, raced back to her room, where she stripped and climbed with all haste into her comfy pajamas and jumped under the bedcovers.

Saturday, 20th December 1958

"I'm sorry you don't feel up to taking the train to London, I'm sure you will miss spending Christmas with your son and his family awfully." Hope said she was sorry, but she was also secretly happy as now Bessie would be joining them for Christmas dinner.

"My arthritis is playing up too much, be far too uncomfortable for me to be rocked for hours by some steam train going far too fast."

They were in the kitchen making mince pies. They'd made the fruit mixture a month ago, soaking it with a large serving of brandy, and the aroma of the ones already in the oven was simply delightful.

Hope had told Bessie, in a whisper because John was in the living room, about the previous night's disaster.

"It can't have been a complete fiasco, I'm sure if he got even a sneaky look at your legs it would have given him something to think upon as he tried to go to sleep."

Hope chuckled. "It took me ages to go to sleep, I was that blooming brassic!"

Bessie chuckled, her portly body shaking up and down. "So I can imagine," she said.

"Are you sure you won't come to church with us tomorrow?"

"I've been away far too long, dear. I couldn't bring myself to face God again after he took my William away from me."

"I'm sure it was Hitler, that did that really," said Hope gently.

"I know, and I've not stopped believing, in fact I still pray every night at bedtime, but I've not been able to face attending church without him by my side."

"Well if I can go, I'm sure you can too."

"Maybe on Christmas Eve, are you going to the Carol Service?"

"Yes, it's the only one I'm looking forward to."

"You didn't enjoy last week's service?"

Hope spooned the minced fruit mixture into the pastry cups. "I don't remember much of it if I'm honest. I think I was so nervous about what the women were saying about me I just went blank."

"I'm sure they have nothing but nice things to say about you," said Bessie kindly.

Hope smiled at her and leaned over to give her a quick hug. "I was surprised last week because we were home much quicker than John normally comes home, it must have been a quick service for some reason."

Bessie threw Hope a puzzled look but didn't say anything.

Sunday, 21st December 1958

The church was chilly, the pews as cold as a dog's nose. Hope put her gloved hands into her coat pockets for extra warmth. John noticed her slight shiver and put his arm around her shoulder to help warm her.

All of a sudden Hope wanted to sing the Hallelujah Chorus! Butterflies danced around her stomach. John was touching her! Despite the 'ground rules' that he had been so adamant about laying down, he was touching her. Warmth flooded through her body that didn't come from clothes or heaters, but from happiness.

When it came time to sing the hymn and they stood up, Hope was bursting with joy. Last week, remembering what Bessie had said about John and Charlotte singing all the time, she'd been unable to join in with the hymns; instead she had mouthed the words. Today, oh but today, she opened up her lungs full belt and sang for all her worth.

John had put his arm around her! He was surely falling in love with her! John cringed when she hit the wrong notes, and Hope took the volume down a little.

She gave the vicar a vigorous handshake as they were leaving, her happiness still conspicuously evident. As they left the entrance and headed towards the walkway John paused. She looked up at him with a question on her face.

"I have to do something Hope, you go on home and I'll be back shortly."

"Sure, see you at home."

John leaned down and kissed her on the cheek.

Hope saw fireworks. Sparkles, glittering and jumping in front of her eyes, how she made it home she would never know. He'd kissed her. He'd kissed her. He'd kissed her!

Chapter 10

Christmas Eve, 1958

RESPECTABILITY BRIMMED UNDER the surface of Hope's skin. With John on one side of her, and Bessie on the other, she was simply bubbling over with joy. The Carol Service was lovely, children held up candles, wafts of frankincense and oranges flooded the pews, and the carols filled everyone present with good cheer. She knew most of them from school days, and as she sang for all she was worth, she knew she'd never been happier in her life.

Her bubble burst shortly after they exited the church. Once again, John kissed her on the cheek and told her he would be home soon. As she walked along with Bessie she was overcome with curiosity and eventually stopped walking.

"Bessie, would you mind walking the rest of the way on your own?"

Bessie looked at Hope and placed her hands on Hope's shoulders. "You know dear, some things are just best left alone."

"I won't be long; I might even catch you up."

"Alright dear, off you go."

Hope hugged Bessie quickly, and then went racing back down towards the church. Twice John had headed to the west side of the church and that's where Hope ran now, her heart pounding.

She slowed as she cornered the church wall and walked towards the graveyard. She didn't have to go far. She spotted John straight away, standing in front of a grave, his head bent, with his hat in his hands.

"Charlotte," whispered Hope, before spinning on her heels and racing away from the resting place of a woman she'd never met but still hated with a passion.

Christmas Day, 1958

Aromas of turkey dinner and Christmas pudding filled the house. John had the BBC playing on the radio fairly loudly in the living room, so they could hear it in the kitchen as the ladies worked together. They were creating a feast fit for a king, no expense had been spared. Bessie had showed Hope how to stuff the turkey, how to honey-coat the parsnips and how to make extra crispy roast potatoes. Although Hope was proud of their hard work, her day was tinged with a gray fog that even the white snow-covered trees outside could do little to erase. She would never be able to compete with a dead woman. She had been a fool to even try.

"I'm wondering if we have time for presents before dinner?" asked John, popping his head around the kitchen door.

"We certainly do," replied Bessie.

Hope smiled, but it didn't reach her eyes.

They went into the living room where their presents sat under the tree. "I'll do the honors," said John, bending down to pick them up.

Bessie insisted they open hers first. She had got them matching leather gloves which must have cost a fair penny.

"You shouldn't have," said Hope getting up and hugging Bessie, "but they are beautiful, thank you so much."

"You're welcome."

"Open ours now," said John, passing Bessie a large box.

As she pulled off the wrapping paper, her pleasure shone through. "I wonder what it is?" she said. Once all the wrappings were off she discovered a box with the gilded inscription of 'E. Schmeckenbecher'. "Oh my! You didn't?" she exclaimed opening the lid with shaking hands.

"Let me help you," said John, lifting out a beautiful cuckoo clock.

"Oh, I've wanted one of those for such a long time," said Bessie clapping her hands.

John and Hope beamed and gave her hugs.

"I can't believe it, I've hinted to my son many a time, that it would please me no end if he could pick up one for me on one of his trips to Europe."

John handed Hope his present to her, and picked up her present to him and sat down to open it. Hope waited for him to open his first, she wanted to catch his expression when he saw what it was so she could gauge if he liked it.

John unwrapped his present and was soon holding a hardback of John Voelker's Anatomy of a Murder in his hands.

"Do you like it? I went to Reid's book shop thinking to pick you up some old books, but I overheard some gentlemen talking about how jolly good they thought Anatomy of a Murder was, and so I changed my mind and bought you that instead."

"I'm sure I will love it, thank you very much."

She blushed slightly, she couldn't tell if he actually loved it, but it was obvious that he liked it.

Hope's hands were shaking as she carefully untied the ribbon around her box. It was quite small and flat, much like a square box of chocolates she thought. Paper aside she saw straight away it wasn't chocolates. It was an old jewelry box. She lifted the lid slowly. Inside, lying on silk padding was a delicate silver necklace, with a rectangle shaped pendant holding a sapphire in the center.

"It's beautiful," she said in a hushed tone as she lifted it out of the box. John got up and came over to her.

"Let me put it on for you," he said taking the necklace from her.

He joined the clasp at the back of her neck. "I know its second hand, but I spotted it in the pawn shop window and I knew straight away that it would look enchanting on you. You don't mind it being second-hand do you?" he asked anxiously, coming around to stand in front of her.

121

"It's the most precious thing I've ever seen," she said with tears trickling down her cheeks. "Thank you." They gave each other an awkward hug. She longed for him to hold her and never let go, but she was resigning herself to the fact that was never going to happen.

Boxing Day was quiet. They had cold turkey sandwiches for supper before turning the television on at six o'clock to tune into the BBC to watch the film The Three Musketeers starring Walter Abel, Paul Lukas and Margot Grahame. They munched on a few Quality Street sweets as they watched. Hope had purchased the tin mostly because of the striking picture on the lid of the loving couple wearing Regency attire; the man in red uniform was striking and the lady in her green dress and bonnet simply delightful.

"I think I prefer the book," said Hope when the film finished.

"You've read Alexandre Dumas?" John couldn't help the surprise in his voice.

"Yes, it was hard going because of the language he uses, but it was so gripping I hated putting it down."

"You do surprise me."

"'Ang on a mo', I ain't no divvy!" Hope declared falling into heavy scouse on purpose.

"Honestly Hope, I never said you were."

"I might have lived in a rough area, but I still went to school… well most of the time."

"OK, OK, pull your neck in. I'm impressed that's all. I've read the Count of Monte Cristo, and although it's a superb story, I struggled with the heavy text myself. So… I'm impressed."

Hope was torn, part of her was indignant for being told to pull her neck in, and part of her was chuffed because he'd complimented her. Blimey, but he was a hard man to live with sometimes. More and more of late she was beginning to feel inferior and useless. She was beginning to get a handle on the whole cooking malarkey, and the house was spotless. But her mind was getting no exercise at all except from reading, and that didn't feel like enough to her.

"I was thinking, in January I'm going to look for a job."

"Over my dead body!"

"What? Are you serious, because maybe I could arrange for your body to be dead?!"

"Don't be ridiculous."

"*Me* ridiculous? You're the one who's just made the most stupid statement ever. If I went to work I could contribute to the housekeeping, you could save more of your salary. I would have thought you would be most pleased by that!"

The wind left John's sails and his body slumped. "I didn't think money was an issue between us Hope. If I don't give you enough money, you need only tell me."

Hope bit her bottom lip. She wanted to stay hopping mad at him, but she couldn't. "I think I'm getting bored, John."

"I thought you enjoyed keeping house?"

"It's not the worst job in the world I have to be honest, but now that we seem to be in full swing of what you consider 'normal' for companions, I find myself longing for something more."

"Oh, I see."

If I had children to look after, or a man to wrap his arms around me during the night I might not be so bored, were the thoughts she bit her tongue not to utter.

"Could we compromise do you think? Could you find a part-time job, for say two days a week?"

Hope had already decided she only wanted to work three days a week, so she smiled. "If that would please you more, then I shall look for a part-time job."

"That's very obliging of you, thank you."

"Would you like another slice of Christmas cake, John?"

And there it was, the classic 'normal' of any married couple, compromise with a slight angle of manipulation. Now if she could only get him to fall in love with her, they truly would be your average married couple.

Joe wasn't hiring and Hope was more than a little deflated. She'd been sure he would have given the job at the garage back to her. She had applied for a few clerical positions, but with no experience or typing skills she wasn't hired.

It seemed only the factories were taking on new people. She could have started straight away if she wanted to be on the conveyer belts at Ogden's tobacco factory. But John had put his foot down on that one, he simply would *not* put up with her coming home stinking of tobacco. It was bad enough that she still sneaked into the back garden to smoke when she thought he wasn't looking. She'd blushed at that, she'd been sure he hadn't noticed. So she had taken a position at Lockwoods sausage factory. However, watching what was put into the massive vats and the constant stink had been enough to make her leave, she'd managed a total of three days before she walked. One thing was for sure, having seen firsthand what went into them, she would never eat a sausage again as long as she lived!

"You're looking glum today, Hope," said the butcher as he wrapped up some lamb chops for her.

"Finding it rather difficult to find a part-time job," she answered with a shrug.

"Is that so? Can you ride a bike?"

"Yes, although it's been years since I have done. Why?"

"Well," said Mr. Whittle nodding towards the big glass window. "My boy has gone off to join the Navy so he has, and the young lad that was going to replace him was caught stealing, so I'm looking for someone to make my deliveries."

Hope glanced where the butcher had looked. Outside the window stood a bike, pitch-black with a huge basket in front of the handlebars, and *Whittle's Family Butchers* painted on a piece of metal between the seat and handle bars. "Are you offering me a job Mr. Whittle?"

"Aye, I'm willing to give you a try if you fancy it?"

In that moment, Mrs. Whittle came into the shop out of the back room, where she must have been listening. "I'm sure the young woman won't want to deliver meat for you, she'll be looking for a much finer job."

While Mr. Whittle was lanky and quite frankly thin as a rake, Mrs. Whittle was a vision of bouncing curvy plumpness, her cheeks round and rosy. As the butcher's wife wiped her hands on her checkered pinafore, Hope realized that the modern, rather expensive clothes she was wearing marked her firmly as middle-class. The thought made her grin. She decided a hint of scouse accent was needed to land this job. Only slightly, so as not to show too much difference between her previous accent and this, Hope laid it on.

"I won't be blagging ya' by tellin' ya' I need the money, 'cos obviously yous can tell," she did a sweeping movement with both her hands over her clothes, "by me clobber, that I ain't short of a bob or two. But it's me better half's money and I wouldn't 'alf like to earn me own." She didn't think she'd 'clucked' too much.

126

Mrs. Whittle still looked unconvinced. "We don't pay much for delivering to them posh houses."

"No we don't," agreed Mr. Whittle. "But if you'd like to give it a go, the job is yours."

His wife frowned at him and put her hands on her hips, obviously not pleased with being overruled.

"It won't hurt our business none if people see a comely young lady like this delivering our wares Mrs. Whittle," he said with a meaningful nod.

"A trial basis then," said his wife.

"Good, it's decided then. Can you start tomorrow?" said the butcher.

"We only pay the boys twelve shillings a day mind," added his wife.

"What time would you like me?" Hope asked with a triumphant smile.

Despite being able to earn an awful lot more in a factory, Hope was more than happy with the suggested pay. If she did three days a week she could save for a rainy day. Besides she would be finishing at one o'clock so it was practically a half day.

She arrived at seven thirty the following morning, eager to begin her new job. The weather was freezing and under her wool trousers and thick knitted jumper she was wearing her thermal vest and winter long-johns.

"You make the deliveries first," said Mrs. Whittle. "Then you come back here and help clean the shop. If we get particularly busy you might be called to help serve the customers too, but not until we know you know all the prices."

"We've written down a list of today's deliveries for you," said the butcher handing her a piece of rough paper. "You start at the top here," he pointed to the first address. "And then make your way down. We've put them in order of distance, so the first one is nearest to the shop, just ten minutes away on the bike."

"Do you know the streets?" asked Mrs. Whittle sharply.

Luckily, Hope had the foresight to ask Bessie last night, and her neighbor had done a rough sketch marking down all the main streets and some smaller ones that housed the toffs, that she was sure would have food delivered.

Hope nodded. "If I'm unsure when I'm out, I'll be sure to stop someone and ask the way."

"Right, well this is heavy, so I'll put it on the bike for you," said Mr. Whittle picking up the huge basket, which was filled with brown paper parcels wrapped with string. Mrs. Whittle tutted and went back to work, leaving them to it.

"Sure you'll be OK Hope?"

She nodded again. The bike did feel heavy, but she was sure she would manage. He left her and went back in the shop. Hope lifted up the support stands in front of the bike and folded them upwards in front of the basket. Then she pointed the bike in the direction of the first house, swung her leg over and mouthed to the skies for help from 'Him up there.' She was off. She wobbled, steadied, made her way along the street and wobbled some more.

Mrs. Whittle tutted behind Mr. Whittle's back as they watched her ride away.

Two successful deliveries later and Hope was brimming with confidence. She could do this, and in the process she would end up super trim and firm. Her posterior might be a bit tender for a couple of weeks, but after that, well everything was grand. The air was freezing and the sky gray threatening snow yet again, but the fresh air was exhilarating and so much better than being cooped up indoors all day.

It was as she was approaching the third 'posh' house that disaster struck. Two black Doberman Pinschers appeared out of nowhere and started chasing the bike. Like well-practiced highwaymen they ran alongside her, one on each side of the bike.

"Go away," she screeched as she kicked out with her right leg to try and put the dog there off getting so close. In response they barked and Hope was both frightened and angry. "Bugger off you damn dogs." They chose to ignore her. In her efforts to outrun them Hope was vaguely aware that she had just gone past the next drop-off point. Kicking out with both legs at the same time, she tried to squeeze on the brake handles to slow the bike down so she could turn around. The road was icy and braking hard turned out to be a mistake. A wobble to the left was corrected and resulted in a wobble to the right. Then time slowed down. The last wobble evolved into a slow diving spin to the right. She crashed into the road, the bike skidded several feet away from her and the brown packages went flying across the road.

If the dogs could talk, they'd be saying 'hee hee hee' and 'thank you kindly' as they each snatched up a brown parcel in their mouths and went charging back down the street.

Hope howled in frustration as she picked herself up.

"Come back 'ere," she screamed in frustration.

Practiced bandits they were, for they didn't slow down. One of the packages had ripped in the dog's mouth, and a trail of sausages flew in the air, bouncing along as they raced for their secret hideout.

"Arrgh!" screeched Hope, as she scrabbled around the road, picking up the packages before either another dog appeared or they got run over.

"You OK miss?" asked a man bending to help pick up packages.

"I'm fine thank you." She wasn't fine; she was cross as a nest of hornets. This was her first day and she was absolutely sure her first day's wages had just gone running off down the street in the jaws of the trickiest robbers she'd ever encountered.

She was right. Even Mrs. Whittle had been slightly sympathetic, but well money is money and they weren't a charity after all. Hope was hugely grateful that she hadn't been fired.

That night when she told John what had happened, expecting some sympathy, he had roared his head off for a full ten minutes.

Chapter 11

DOUGLAS HAD BROUGHT TWO FRIENDS with him and Hope had her nose put out of joint. She was pleased that her brother had made good friends with the other sailors, but she had so been looking forward to spending some time with him. Her disappointment was not to end there, for he was just explaining how he was off to Wales to see Betty for a week.

Hope was crushed that he was giving her a flying visit while he was giving Betty a whole week. She was also hurt that Betty had been writing to Douglas but not to her.

"I didn't realize the two of you weren't in contact anymore, why don't you come to Wales for a holiday with me?"

"I don't think so, she's made it clear she doesn't want anything to do with me anymore and I have no idea why."

An odd expression on Douglas's face gave Hope the impression that he knew why. She cocked her head to the side and gave a Douglas a 'what' look.

"She was always jealous of you sis."

"Don't be daft, what on earth has she got to be jealous about?"

"Don't pretend like you don't know you're the pretty one."

Hope looked shocked. "No I'm not, she's the one who inherited ma's lovely long legs, and lush red hair, she's the cracker not me."

Douglas's two friends took a drink of their tea at the same time and raised their eyebrows at each other over the brim of their cups.

"You're beautiful you daft thing. You might be pint-sized but you're beautiful, especially when you put on your best clobber an all. Anyway, it's not only the looks, you also got your dad's brains. Betty could never hold down a good job like you could, her lot in life was always going to be the factory. And the icing on the cake? Look where you've landed, you couldn't have done anything better to make her spitting-mad with jealousy."

Here, Hope had to agree with him. She was deeply grateful for the life of comfort she now lived in. She knew she would never take 'not being hungry' for granted. An empty stomach teaches you to appreciate things like nothing else can.

"Look, I'll come back and visit you when I return from Wales, OK?"

Hope nodded, what else could she do?

"Look what I've got you," said Douglas going into his duffle bag.

Hope unwrapped a roughly covered box. The box was dirty and dog-eared and she wondered what on earth he'd got her.

"Don't worry about the box, the gift didn't come in a box so I used an old one I had," said Douglas.

Hope lifted out a beautiful Japanese geisha doll.

"It's a music box," said one of Douglas's friends. "You wind her up at the back of the box."

Hope smiled at him, and then looked at Douglas with water in her eyes. "She's beautiful," she said. "Thank you."

The doll's white china face looked so delicate. The details were amazing, the delicate umbrella she had so real looking.

"So you went to Japan?" she asked as she wound her up on the back.

"Yes, we've been all over. That reminds me…" Douglas fished in his bag again and bought out a pile of postcards. "I promised you these," he said handing the cards to her. "I wasn't sure where you were for a long time so I wrote them and kept them for you."

Tears trickled down her cheeks, Douglas had been thinking of her all this time after all.

After Douglas and his friends had left, Hope became despondent. Her body slumped like a balloon losing its air. She'd always looked up to Betty, true, she had been jealous of Betty too when ma had bought her gifts and taken her dancing with her. But at night when Hope had woken with her nightmares, it had been Betty who'd wrapped her arm around her and comforted her.

Life in the slums for the main part had been harsh. Hunger had been the worst. But what they'd had together as siblings had been priceless. They'd stood together to face the world, four gallant soldiers facing adversity with love and loyalty as their shields. Part of her missed those days, but only a small part.

Douglas never made it back to visit Hope before he boarded ship for his next voyage. He wrote a long letter though telling her how sorry he was, it was just time had gone so quickly and he'd met a young woman called Shirley and he'd wanted to spend as much time with her as possible.

Hope understood, but still she hurt inside.

He'd also written to tell her that Betty and Fred were now married and had a baby boy called Joseph. Fred had a respectable job and was a factory floor manager, the job came with a house and so they were comfortable. Hope had been glad to hear that good news. He also enclosed Betty's address and told Hope that she should consider writing to her.

Hope placed his letter in her wooden keep-sake box next to his other letters and pile of postcards. She had no intention of writing to Betty, although she did wish her well.

Chapter 12

Saturday, 8th March 1959

EVER INCREASING CONCERN OVER HOPE'S mood dominated John's thoughts every day. Was she sinking even as Charlotte had done? All he'd wanted was a little company, and maybe someone to look after him, he hadn't been prepared to be so attuned to Hope's feelings and moods. He was beginning to realize that there was nothing simple about their arrangement.

Inside him he knew that Hope loved him. It was written over every expression she made, whether it was happy or sad he knew he was the one causing her mood swings and deepening depression. Of course she would want more than someone to talk to; she was a young vibrant woman, so loving and sweet. So pretty, so feminine. He sighed. He couldn't pretend it wasn't happening anymore, either he 'fix' her, or he would have to ask her to leave – for her own good. He sucked in his breath and let out an exaggerated sigh. Lord, but he didn't want to lose her. He'd grown accustomed to the chatterbox. Her cooking had become decidedly tasty, and she had picked up her spirits a little after starting work at the butchers. But there was no mistaking the cloud of gloom that hung over her these days.

To cheer her up he planned a visit to the Jacaranda as he knew she loved it there. The Hy-Tones were playing this evening and he was sure she would enjoy their modern music; it wasn't his cup-of-tea but he understood it would be Hope's. Music was one of the constant reminders of their age gap.

He'd been right. Hope came alive as soon as he told her they were going. When she walked down the stairs all dressed up, John caught his breath. She wore a black, tight-fitting turtleneck sweater, with a full midi-length black and red checkered skirt, and black sling-back court shoes. She had a new red headband on her head and carried a little square red purse. But it was her face that John was glued to. She looked amazing. Black kohl-lined eyelids, brown eye shadow and red lipstick, transformed her from a young lass into a beautiful, very appealing woman. He was floored by the transformation.

She couldn't help smiling shyly at his expression, 'gob-smacked' her ma would have said. She took each stair slowly and deliberately. With Bessie's help she had been planning this 'new look' for a long time. She was 'hip' and attractive, and for the first time in her life she knew it. Now… if only John could see her as a woman instead of a companion.

"You look stunning," he said.

"You look particularly dapper yourself Mr. Walker," she said when she reached the hallway. Indeed he did, he was wearing his plain black Sunday suit, white shirt and black tie. The attire suited him well and he looked rather handsome.

Just then there was a knock on the door.

"That will be the taxi," John said, and pulled his eyes off her with difficulty. She couldn't help the cute grin that appeared on her face as he turned around.

"One moment," he said to the taxi driver. The driver tipped his cap and headed back to the car.

John took Hope's coat off the stand and held it open for her. As she slipped her arms into it she was awash with the feeling of being treated like a proper lady, and she liked it tremendously! This was endorsed when he held open the taxi door for her. Once she was inside he shut the door and raced around the car to get in the other side.

Luckily, John had been in earlier and booked them a table, because the place was heaving. They pushed their way through the crowd and John pulled out a chair for her to sit down. Boy she felt special; she was also longing for a smoke but didn't want to spoil the magical evening by smoking in front of him.

They hadn't been there long when the Hy-tones came on, all dressed in white suits with black shirts. From the moment the first note struck Hope sat up straight on the edge of her seat glued to the performance, her feet tapping along to the music. As they finished each song she jumped up, clapped and cheered like mad. John sat back in his chair and enjoyed watching her.

When they took a break and the room was a little quieter, Hope leaned across the table. "Thank you so much for bringing me."

"You're welcome, I'm just sorry it's been such a while since we've been here. We'll come more often I promise."

That was sweet-music to Hope's ears. She excused herself and headed towards the powder room on a complete high.

"Oops sorry," she said as she bumped into someone in the hallway on the way to the bathrooms.

"Hope?"

She looked up and nearly fell over when her heart did a summersault in her ribs.

Strong arms reached out and grabbed her arms to steady her.

She moved backwards until her back was pressed against the wall. Her heart was pounding so hard she thought she might be having a heart-attack.

"Hope?"

"Hello Ted."

They were silent for a full minute as they looked at each other. Hope was trying to work out why she felt so sick, so bereft so… heartbroken.

"You look beautiful," said Ted, not for a second taking his eyes away from hers.

Why did she long for him to take her in his arms? Why did the dream of kissing him abruptly come to mind, and why was it so real and passionate? She wanted him. All of

138

her wanted all of him. She wanted to drown in his eyes. She wanted to turn back time.

Then she remembered standing outside the picture house for over two hours.

"I'm married," she blurted.

His face fell and she knew he'd taken the news as harshly as she meant it.

"I looked for you."

"What?"

"After that Friday when I didn't show, I went everywhere I could think you might show up. For months I looked for you. I waited outside Vernons' doors at night for weeks until one day a woman asked me why I was there. She told me you'd left ages ago. After that I walked the streets of Wavertree trying to see you."

"It would have been easier if you had just shown up at the picture house."

He crumbled in front of her, she felt a tiny pang of regret, but before he could continue she pushed herself off the wall and straightened up.

"It's been just ducky seeing you Ted, but I must go. Take care." And with that she turned and went into the powder room. She thought he might have been waiting for her when she came out but he was gone and she breathed a sigh of relief.

The evening had been tarnished though, she tried to cover it up but John saw. After half-an-hour had passed he asked her if she wanted to go home and she nodded eagerly. He never asked her what was wrong, and for that she was grateful. Ted was her secret, one she wanted to bury and never think of again.

———⚜———

As the following months flew by John became increasing concerned for Hope. She still smiled, but it never reached her eyes anymore. She talked less and less and went to bed early to avoid sitting with him in the living room. They used to sit in there and read, they might not have been talking all the time, just an occasional interjection to share something they had read, but it was comfortable, homely, very… companionable.

He missed her. Hope was still there in body, but her mind had left him – just like Charlotte's had done. He was at his wits end when Bessie suggested that he take her on holiday. 'The fresh air of the country was what the young thing needed to perk her up,' Bessie had said.

Hope had announced a few weeks before that she wasn't going to work for the butchers anymore, when John had asked if she planned to find something else she said, 'what for?' Her malady was draining the life out of her, he had to do something.

John decided to discuss a holiday with Hope and see what she thought.

"I've been thinking," he said as they finished their evening meal and moved into the living room. "I think it would be good for us to go away on a holiday, what do you think? Our wedding anniversary is coming up at the beginning of October, so I was thinking, why don't we go away for two weeks, the last week of September and the first of October?"

"That would be a nice change, what do you have in mind?"

"Well, if it's alright with you, I'd actually like to go back to a farm in Wales that the family used to holiday at when I was a young lad. I've written them a letter to see if they still rent out the cottage and they do, and it is available on the dates I suggested. I haven't booked it yet though; I wanted to be sure you were happy with the choice before I did."

"That's thoughtful of you John. I would be happy to go to Wales with you."

"Oh jolly good! We have several cars at work which we use when doing surveys, I've been told it is acceptable for me to borrow one of them for the two weeks, so we can drive there."

"How lovely!"

"Are you being sarcastic?"

Hope chuckled. "No. I'm not. I was thinking how marvelous it is because now I will be able to take a ton of clothes with me."

"Oh, I don't think the boot is particularly big," said John, his face flushing. "Also, the cottage is in the middle of nowhere so you won't need much stuff, mainly walking boots for hiking. I mean it's really a holiday for simply switching off, maybe having a whiskey in the evening and reading a good book. I don't even think they have television in there yet, although I know they have a jolly good radio."

"It's alright, I'm just joking with you."

"Oh," he said pretending to wipe sweat off his forehead.

Hope picked her book off the coffee table and started towards the door. "I think I'll call it a day, night John."

He stood as she went to move. He wanted very much to take her in his arms and comfort her. "I hope the country air will do much to revive your constitution," he said as she was leaving.

"Pardon?" she stopped and turned around.

He could see by her face that he had said the wrong thing.

"It's just I think it would be good for both of us to get away for a while, don't you think?"

"Goodnight John." She turned and left him to his feelings of inadequacy, but at least she had agreed to go away with him, he'd half been expecting her to decline.

Chapter 13

Saturday, 26th September 1959

HOPE WAS SO EXCITED she felt like a child again. When John had announced they should go on a holiday she'd instantly hoped for somewhere exciting like Bournemouth or even Paris, so when he'd said he wanted to rent a cottage in Wrexham, Wales, she'd been disappointed. Now, however, she was full of excitement.

The drive from Liverpool to Wrexham was a pure delight. Hope had fair leaned out of the window the entire way. 'You're like a puppy,' John had laughed at her.

She felt young and excited. This was their first holiday. Sometimes she found it hard to believe a year had passed and they were still together. Nearly every day she expected him to turn around and announce he couldn't do it anymore and she had to leave. The fear of being rejected again crippled her spirits. Like a flower being denied water, she felt herself wilting with no idea how to stop the fall.

This holiday, she had resolved, was to be a magic-encased time capsule, where for two weeks she wouldn't allow herself to worry about either her past or her future, not even for one single minute. She was determined to have a lovely holiday.

It seemed John was similarly resolved, for he turned on the radio and the two of them sang their hearts out, one song after another until they were parched. It took them slightly over two hours, but finally they were driving around Wrexham and heading towards the small village of Minera.

"I thought we'd stop off at the Tyn-Y-Capel for some lunch before going to the cottage," John said, pulling the dark grey Austin into the inn's car park. As the sun was shining and it was warm, they decided to sit in the gardens and absorb the stunning, lush greens of the countryside. In the distance they could hear the bubbling flow of the River Clywedog.

Hope sighed. "This was such a good idea, John."

He brimmed with contentment at her approval.

They had scampi and chips, washed down with homemade lemonade. They didn't talk much. They simply sat together enjoying the food and the views. It was so peaceful.

After lunch John drove them straight to the cottage, quite pleased (and slightly amazed) at himself for remembering the way. He had studied his leather bound AA Road Atlas the night before, but still he felt like he'd found his way there more by instinct than planning.

The cottage was just as John had remembered it. White painted stone walls, with a gray slate roof. Behind it was a small copse and the deep green of the trees seemed to emphasize the white walls.

"It's so picturesque," said Hope, getting out of the car.

"I agree with you, it is very quintessentially English. Let's go in, I'll fetch the bags later. The door should be open."

Hope turned the handle and sure enough the door swung open. "They don't lock it up," she whispered in surprise.

"I think they do when it isn't going to be used for a while. And there should be a key on the inside of the door. But I guess they're so far from anyone they have no fear of burglary."

It was so quaint. Totally original features gave it character and warmth, while a couple of modern pieces (namely a cooker and a refrigerator) helped to make it more modern.

"I wouldn't have expected a refrigerator out here," said Hope as she opened the door to look inside. On the shelves were eggs, milk, a cooked ham, cheese and butter. "Look at this food," she exclaimed, "is it for us?"

"Yes. I imagine some people like to come here for a while and not see another living soul for a week or two. So being able to stock up is extremely handy. A lot of walkers come here to embrace the hills and fresh air of Wales."

"That sounds awfully energetic of them!" laughed Hope.

"Indeed it does."

"I'm going to take a peek upstairs." Before John could answer she was charging up the tiny stone staircase. "There are only two rooms up here, John," she called as she walked into the first one.

It was the master bedroom. A huge rug lay over the bare floorboards, a cross hung on the wall over the bed, and the bed was covered in a multi-colored crocheted bedspread. It was small and simple, but spotless and homely. She walked into the other bedroom and was surprised to see that it had two small beds in it, neither of which had been made up.

She went back downstairs. "There's no bathroom, John?"

He chortled. "It's downstairs, behind the kitchen, bathroom and toilet."

"Phew!" she pretended to wipe sweat from her forehead. "But there's only one room prepared upstairs, do I have to make it up myself? Do you know where the linen is kept?"

John flushed red, and coughed. "I, umm, I meant to tell you…"

"What?"

"I told them to only make up the master bedroom."

"You did?"

His cheeks were now burning like hot coals. "Umm, yes I did."

Hope looked confused.

"Look Hope," he came over and grabbed her hands in his. She looked up at him. "I thought, I mean if it is acceptable with you, I thought, I mean, we could…"

"Sleep in the same bed?"

Air came whistling out of John's lungs. "Yes, exactly, what do you think?"

It was a shock, but most definitely a pleasant one. "I'm quite happy with the situation," she answered with a soft smile.

"Good stuff. Well then, I might as well fetch the bags."

Hope helped bring their few belongings in. They unpacked, and then headed off for a short walk down the tiny country lane so that John could show Hope where the farmhouse was, and introduce her to their temporary landlords. No one had been at home, but at least Hope now knew where it was. Hope had slipped her hand into John's on the way home and he hadn't knocked it away.

Later, they turned on the radio and opened a bottle of wine. They sliced some of the huge farmhouse loaf they'd found in the cupboard and cut thin pieces of the ham and cheese and set everything on the table in the tiny living room.

"Shall I light the fire?" John asked as they were about to eat. "There are logs ready to use if we want one."

"No, let's leave it for tonight, maybe tomorrow?" In her mind she was thinking being cold might be a good reason to go to bed early!

As it happened they enjoyed the radio, wine and nibbles, and relaxed in each other's company for a few hours before Hope finally stretched and said she was ready for bed.

As he watched her climb the stairs John did wonder whether Hope had brought her flannelette pajamas or her small baby-doll nightie.

Unfortunately, so Hope was thinking, she had only brought the pajamas. She had assumed it would be cold at night, and she was right. She was glad for their warmth as she slipped between the fresh linen sheets.

Her heart beat terribly hard, when she heard John climb the stairs.

He'd put his pajamas on downstairs, so he turned off the light and got straight into bed. They both lay on their backs looking at the ceiling.

"It's a long way to go if we need a widdle in the night," remarked Hope after a while of silence.

"I could fetch a bucket for you if you like?"

"Certainly not!" Hope had grown up with a 'family' bucket placed in the middle of the bedroom so they didn't have to go out into the garden at night to use the toilet. But she'd always hated it, and there was no way on earth she was doing that now.

There was so much she wanted to ask him, mainly why had he decided to do this now, after all this time. But in the end she asked him. "Would it be alright if I cuddled you?"

"Yes," he answered in a husky voice.

She couldn't tell if he really wanted her to or not, but she didn't know if tomorrow he would still want this, so she grabbed her opportunity by turning on her side and slipping her arm around him. She gave a contented sigh, and amazingly was asleep within five minutes.

It took John much longer before his body unwound and allowed him to sleep.

148

They were both surprised to discover that walking was something they actually enjoyed rather a lot. They couldn't have picked better weather, and with long dry sunny days they were able to walk for hours in the day, returning back to the cottage exhausted but extremely happy.

John hadn't asked her to make up the spare bed which filled her with joy, but what thrilled her even more was when on the second night he had lay back against the pillow and put out his arm to hold her. She had snuggled into his chest and thought she would die of happiness.

They had three perfect days of harmony before the fireworks started.

Later, neither of them would be able to remember exactly how it started, but they had their first full-blown fallout on the evening of the fourth day.

"You'll never love me like you loved her!" Hope accused.

"I never said I would, I never said I would love you. We had an arrangement, it was good. We were to be companions. But you… you… with all your lovely doe-eyes, and gentle ways and your… your… sweet voice."

"What's wrong with my voice?" Hope screeched.

"You never quit talking! I just wanted somebody quiet to join me for dinner in the evenings. I didn't advertise for a chatter-box!"

"I thought you never advertised in the end?"

"Well, I didn't. But you know what I mean. Stop being so God damn irritable and womanly-like."

149

"I am a woman you moron."

He went slightly blue in the face and she thought that maybe she had crossed his barrier of sensitivities, and decided to back down a little. She knew what was causing this fire of emotions inside her. It was due to lying next to the man she loved at night and for wanting more than to just sleep beside him.

"Hope, I can't give you what you want." He collapsed into the sofa. "I am a terrible man, an awful person, a dreadful husband. I killed my first wife and I can't bear the thought of killing you too."

"What?"

He looked at her face, which was completely shocked.

"Not in the way you're obviously thinking. I killed her through neglect, by not understanding her pain."

She joined him on the sofa and took his hand.

"Tell me, John."

And so he began, pouring out his pain and tormented soul.

"This body may be the same, but my mind has been forever changed by war. Far into history has my innocence faded, destroyed by visions of horror scratched into my mind, embedded in my soul. I was twenty-three when the war started twenty-nine when it ended, but I felt more like eighty-nine. I asked Charlotte to be patient with me, to let her gentle kindness steer us when fits of uncontrollable anger suffocated me. Rage overwhelmed me and left me less of a man. My contemporaries didn't understand my lack of strength. Do you know how hard it was to appear stoic after everything I'd seen? But so locked was I within my tortured soul that I did not see her! I didn't notice my beautiful Charlotte as she sank into despair. Maybe, if it had just been my problems that she dealt with, she would have buoyed back up, resurfaced with strength. But two miscarriages turned out to be one-too-many. To my shame, I did get glimpses of something lurking beneath her smile, hiding in the back of her eyes, but I turned away. I was too engrossed in my own misery and scars to want to face her depression. I failed her…" John's voice broke.

Hope moved closer to comfort him but he held up his hand to bid her stay where she was. He would not be able to go on if she came too close. Her kindness would break his walls and she'd see him crumble, he couldn't have that.

"I let my hatred of war, caused by that unspeakable curse which is helplessness, take a hold of me. I am visited everyday by the faces of my comrades who didn't return. They're not accusing, and yet *I* am guilt-ridden for the fact that God chose to smile down upon me, for I returned when they did not. As you know, I was a pilot in the R.A.F. Many bombers went out only some of us came back. We were statistics to the War Ministry propaganda merchants but to us pilots and other aircrew in the R.A.F. we're real people, with families and lives to return."

"What happened was a terrible thing, I cannot begin to imagine the pain your carry, but this thought occurs to me," said Hope, leaning forward and at last placing a hand upon his knee. "For those few who did return, don't the dead urge you all to live? Don't they rise from their pits of darkness and cry out to you who returned – live, live well, and live for those of us who cannot? Wouldn't the fact that you can't enjoy life bring them more sorrow than the fact that they themselves cannot laugh and love? Should you not show your gratitude for their sacrifice by enjoying the life granted to you?"

John's face was ashen, Hope's words pierced his eardrums but did not seem to reach his mind.

"She took her own life."

"Who?"

"Charlotte. She took an evening ferry across the Mersey, and jumped when they were halfway over. It took the police three days to find her body."

"Oh John, I'm so sorry."

"On the 15th of each month I ride the ferry to remember the torture she must have been in to make her jump."

"Oh John," she went to hold him, but he held her off.

"I'm a terrible husband Hope, undeserving of your love. I can't be what you want me to be. I can't be your knight upon a white horse."

"Would you let me sink then, even as Charlotte did? How much better it would have been for me, if you had let me jump off that blasted ferry that night!"

Smack!

He had no idea how it happened, or even really why, but all at once John's hand had shot out and slapped Hope harshly across the face.

"Aah!!" Hope flew backwards into the sofa, her hand raised to her face instinctively.

It took only three seconds for John to realize what he'd done. "Hope!" he reached for her, but she pulled away, jumped up and ran from the room. He stood and called after her. "Hope, Hope, I'm sorry."

He listened to her hasty footfall on the stairs, and then when the bedroom door slammed he sank back onto the sofa, burying his face in hands. "What have I done? Oh God, what have I done?"

The house was silent except for the sniffles that come with crying. John's head in his hands, Hope's buried in a pillow. Eventually, even the gasps of after-crying ceased.

In the silence John prayed, beseeched and begged the Lord to help him. He was lost. He didn't know what to do. He needed guidance. "Help me God," he begged.

He felt a stirring of life in his heart, the heart he thought he had shut down for good. He sat in the silence and began to thank God for His answer.

"John?"

John startled, he hadn't heard her come back downstairs. He looked up, his face distraught, full of pain. He stood up, shaking like a leaf in the wind. "Hope, I'm so sorry. Please forgive me, please."

Hope crossed the room and when she was close enough he pulled her into his arms, where she pressed in close and laid her face against his chest. They stood in silence for a few moments, their closeness already beginning to heal the pain the pair of them carried like lead in their hearts.

After a while, John pulled back slightly so that he could cup Hope's face in his hands. "That was unforgivable of me."

"John," the tears started again, she couldn't help them, they slipped from the corner of her eyes and trickled down her cheeks. "It's not the slap that hurt; it's the fact that you don't love me."

"I…" John interrupted.

"No, hush now," Hope put a finger against his lips. "Thank you for explaining things to me, at least now I can stop tormenting myself and putting myself down with thoughts of how awful I am."

"You're not…"

"Shush, John. It's my turn. Let's sit down."

They sat and turned to face each other.

"You were straight with me from the start, you only wanted a companion. It's my own silly fault that I let myself fall in love with you. In future I will be more careful to pay attention to what people are saying, and to remember that it's not up to me to change them. I wanted to make you happy, I really did. But I grew to want more. More than conversation and company, I wanted… I want… a husband."

She could see that John was controlling his urge to interrupt, biting his tongue so that she could say her piece.

"You've been nothing but kindness itself to me, but I don't think I can stay with you anymore. It's too painful. I've got to leave John, try and get a life for myself somewhere else."

"No!" John shook his head most emphatically. This couldn't happen now! God had only just shown him the way. "No. I've been a fool, I won't lose you Hope. I want you to stay with me. I want you to give me one more chance. Please?"

"I can't compete with Charlotte, I understand now that she has, and always will have, your heart. You need to let me go so that I can search for that someone who will love me with the same passion that you love Charlotte."

"You have to give me another chance, don't leave me. Please don't leave me."

Their eyes were locked in a tangible way, like lovers caressing. His blue-gray eyes were pleading, her hazel eyes unsure.

"Stay." He could see a million thoughts racing through her eyes. "Give me six months, if you still want to leave after that I'll help you pack your bags."

She couldn't help the smile that touched her lips and eyes. "Alright, six months, you have a deal." She offered him her hand, which he took, but instead of shaking it, he raised it to his lips and kissed it. A shiver ran through her body, a thrill, a hope, and maybe a spark of a promise.

Later that night as Hope lay sleeping peacefully her head upon his chest; John prayed that he would be able to make her happy. He wasn't in love with her, not like he had been with Charlotte, but the thought of losing her company tore at him. Thoughts of going back to his lonely life hovered around his spirit, like vultures around carrion. His arm

155

tightened around her sleeping body. She had become dear to him, he cared for her and he knew life would become unbearable again without her.

Early the next morning, Hope set off and enjoyed the mile-long walk to the farm. She'd left before John had risen and before the heat of the day kicked in. They'd both found it hard to sleep and today would have to be a lazy, relaxing day, but they needed some refreshments. Birdsong echoed down the narrow path that led to the farm. It was going to be a glorious day, she could tell. The rich green hedgerows teemed with life. Rabbits hopped off the path into the hedge as they heard her approach, but not before she'd seen them. Herb-Robert crept between the hedgerows, its mauve petals throwing splashes of color everywhere. Lining the path on both sides, purple Harebell grew in abundance. It was beautiful and Hope bubbled over with joy and peace.

At a gate opening in the hedgerow, she stopped and looked in at a field that had become a forest of dark green supporting a wave of brightest yellow. The sunflowers towered above her, making her feel small. Hoverflies and butterflies fluttered from flower to flower. For some reason she was stirred by the sight and sounds. The vicar's sermon from her last visit to church sprang to mind... *Look at the lilies and how they grow, they don't work or make their clothing, yet Solomon in all his glory was not dressed as beautifully as they were. (Luke 12:27).*

"Maybe, if God allows such awful things into the world he sprinkles beauty too, to ease the pain of suffering, like little traces of hope." She shook her head to clear her thoughts. Was she beginning to believe?

"Good morning!" hailed the farmer's wife as Hope approached the farmhouse. "Is everything fine at the cottage?"

"Oh yes, Mrs. Walsh it's truly wonderful. I've never known such peacefulness; it sometimes takes my breath away."

"Please call me Beca. Aww, 'tis a little piece of Heaven for sure. So what can I do for you today?"

"John says I can buy some more produce from you, we definitely need some bread and butter if you have any for sale?"

"'Tis the farmer's market next week, so we are well stocked up, come on in and fill a basket."

Hope followed Beca into an outhouse that had racks stocked with various foodstuffs.

"Fill the basket, my love, John can settle up at the end of the holiday."

"Thank you." Hope filled her basket with sour-dough bread and lots of salad items. At the back of the room was a rack of cheeses. "What's this?" she called back to Beca who was boxing vegetables at the entrance.

"Our best seller that is, like cheddar cheese but laced with mustard seeds and a good portion of ale in the mixture. It's incredibly creamy with a kick from the seeds."

"Oh, I think John will love that."

When she'd finished, Beca took note of the things in the basket and the cost.

"The field of sunflowers is so beautiful, I think if I was a painter I would love to sit for hours and paint them."

"That's the truth, indeed. 'Tis beautiful they are, they're so useful to us too, they help fill the coffers and keep us going, even when other crops fail."

"Really?"

"Oh yes, they're a blessing from God himself they are. Do you know they follow the sun? Not now like, but as they grow, overnight they turn their heads to the East so they can catch the rays, then they slowly move during the day so they are facing west when the sun sets. One of those little miracles I love about nature."

"But they don't do that now?"

"No, when they're full grown they stop turning, but they all face east, each and every one of them. They might be too old to move much but because they warm up quickly each morning they catch the pollinators. Lessen in there somewhere for us folk who are getting on. They're proper name is Helianthus, from Helios which means the sun in Greek."

"I didn't know that. There was just something so… I don't know, I can't seem to find the right word."

"Hopeful? Joyful?"

"Yes, both those."

"I've always found yellow to be the color of hope, and when they're full grown the sight of them always fills me with joy, year after year. You pick a few on your way back, there's a vase under the sink back at the cottage."

"Thank you, I appreciate that, they're so lovely."

"Take the goods home in the basket, just bring it back when you next come around."

"Thanks, I will."

Back at the field Hope picked three sunflowers. She couldn't wait to get back and show them to John.

Chapter 14

THE THREE SUNFLOWERS ON THE TABLE looked striking.

As Hope stood back to admire them in the vase, John came behind her and wrapped his arms around her waist. Her whole body became a mass of fireworks.

"Morning," he said planting a kiss on the top of her head. "Scrambled eggs on toast for breakfast?"

"Good idea. I've got some fresh ones from the farm. They were still warm when I put them in the basket. I'll do them now, it won't take long."

"My turn to cook. You go and sit down."

Hope had a puzzled smile on her face, but shrugged. "OK then."

When breakfast was almost ready, Hope made them a pot of tea and set the table. She didn't remove the flowers, just pushed them to one side.

"Thank you," she said as John put a plate in front of her. "I must admit I'm famished."

As they were eating, Hope asked. "What do you think of the flowers? Aren't they beautiful? Beca says she believes they're flowers of hope."

"They are lovely, but they're not as beautiful as you."

Hope's hand stopped midway between her mouth and the plate. Her heart was beating so fast. Something had changed. She lowered her fork and put it back down without eating. She had suddenly lost her appetite.

No words passed between them, but they knew. Electricity sparked as they reached out to touch each other's hands.

They stood.

They moved closer together.

She tilted her head.

He cupped her face in his hands.

And then their lips were together.

Gentle.

Searching.

Then they were lost in each other.

Pain melted away, emotions sparked to life, and for the first time since their wedding day they truly became husband and wife.

"It's just occurred to me?" Hope said as they walked across the farmer's path holding hands. "You never were going to jump were you?"

He squeezed her hand slightly. "No."

"Then why did you pretend you were going to?"

"It felt like you were unsure about jumping. I thought if you had to rescue me that night, then you would never guess that I had set out to rescue you!"

"So, you've really been my knight in shining armor all along."

John stopped walking and picking Hope up swung her round and round in big circles.

She laughed in delight.

When he put her down he reached up to gently touch her face with the back of his hand. "Are you happy?"

"Extremely."

"Then you have your answer, I must indeed be that shining knight."

They continued on their way.

"I'm going to take the sunflowers home with us. Beca says I can leave the seeds in newspaper during the winter and plant them in February, next year we will have our own hope flowers growing in our garden."

Chapter 15

Saturday, 10th October 1959

"THERE'S NO NEED TO TELL ME, DEAR, I can tell by your face."

"Oh, Bessie I'm so happy I could bust a gut!"

"I'm that pleased for you dear, I really am." They hugged for ages. Eventually, Bessie patted Hope on the back. "Come on, let's have a brew and you can tell me all about it."

Pot of tea made, the pair sat in Bessie's comfy kitchen at the table as Hope poured everything out, including the argument and the make-up afterwards.

"You know my grandmother had a saying," said Bessie.

"What was that?"

"That women can talk themselves in and out of love."

"I don't get that," said Hope with furrowed eyebrows.

"I believe she was right. If a woman wants to be in love with a man it isn't long before she believes that she is, but she could just as easy talk herself out of it too. Say something often enough it has a habit of coming true." Bessie was looking at Hope as if trying to impart a big secret.

"You don't think I really love John?"

163

"I think it is very easy to confuse emotions. Take a desire for security or a need to be wanted; they are both easily mistaken for love."

"I love John, I really do."

Bessie leant over and patted Hope's hand. "I'm absolutely sure you think you do."

"But…"

Bessie put her hand up to cut her off.

"Come on lass, let's bake up a storm. I know your anniversary was last week, but let's celebrate tomorrow. We'll have a full roast with all the trimmings and a choice of cakes that would make the best French patisserie chef weep!"

Hope frowned, she had an urge to argue with her friend and explain how much John meant to her, but somehow she couldn't find the right words, so she shrugged instead.

"OK, I'll let John know what we're doing and ask him to pop to the butchers for a piece of prime roasting beef. Shall we cook the roast in our house?"

"Sure, and we'll cook all the cakes here today at mine."

After the church service, John kissed Hope on the cheek. "Are you sure you don't mind?"

She took hold of his hand and squeezed it tightly. "No John, I don't mind. Seriously I don't. I understand that you love Charlotte – well the memory of her, I would never ask you to give that up. Go and give her your weekly update, I'm sure she missed you these last two weekends."

John gave them a wave as Hope and Bessie set off for home.

He had mixed emotions about visiting the grave today. From the moment he had first met Charlotte he had shared everything with her. Since her suicide he had continued to pour his heart out to her, although now she could no longer reply.

The bench was wet, so he decided to stand, despite the cold damp air he removed his hat and held it in front of him.

"Hello my love, I have something to tell you. I never thought it would happen to me again, but I've fallen in love. I know I told you the marriage was for companionship only, but she worked her way into my heart. She was so sad Charlotte, so desperate to be loved. And I couldn't help myself, she is so sweet and funny, oh and oh so chatty. You'd love her, I know you would. I'm sure the two of you could have been great friends. Don't think badly of me my darling. You'll always have a piece of my heart."

John fell quiet, not too sure how to decipher what was going on inside him. "I wish you could give me a sign, something to let me know we have your blessing."

He moved from foot to foot to try and keep warm. How quickly the weather had turned this year. When they had left Wales the sun had been shining, but before they'd reached home a storm had blown in and it hadn't warmed up since.

John heard the crunch on gravel as someone approached. "How you doing, Mr. Walker?"

"Hello young man, I'm remarkably well actually. And how are you? Have you found yourself a belle yet?"

"Nar, I've not been looking if I'm honest."

"What's that you've got there?" said John pointing to something wrapped in newspaper in the young man's arms.

The young man pulled his cap firmly down with one hand and shuffled slightly. "Well actually Mr. Walker, I knows' how you like to keep the grave looking ship-shape and I noticed you hadn't been for a couple of weeks. So, we had some flowers left over from yesterday's funeral that no one wanted. And as soon as I saw these sunflowers, I thought to myself, they'd look right proper they would on Mrs. Walker's grave. So, I was going to lay them here for her, and for you."

"Sunflowers?"

"Yes I know they're unusual for a funeral, apparently the old lady who died used to love them though. It were 'er sister who brought them along. But before she left she told me to take them as she suddenly couldn't stand the thought of seeing them wilt on her sister's grave. So, here I am."

John looked at Charlotte's grave, could this be a sign? "Very thoughtful of you, please go ahead and put them down."

166

The flowers were taken out of the paper and laid across the grave.

"Ted, I would like for you to meet my wife. Why don't you come home with me now and have Sunday dinner with us? Our neighbor Bessie and my wife have been cooking for two solid days; we're in for a feast. It's a belated anniversary celebration, what say you?"

"I think that'd be swell, Mr. Walker, thanks very much. Can we go passed my house first so I can wash and change and let me dad know I'm off out?"

"Of course."

A short while later John opened the front door and ushered Ted inside. The delicious aroma of dinner engulfed them straight away.

"Ladies, I've brought a guest for dinner, I hope that's alright," called John as they made their way to the kitchen.

Hope was at the stove stirring the gravy. She didn't turn around as she called out. "It's fine, we've got enough here to feed an army."

"And who do we have here?" asked Bessie, wiping her hands on her apron.

"This is Ted. Ted this is our neighbor Bessie, and at the stove is my wife Hope."

"Pleased to meet you young man," said Bessie.

"Pleased to meet you," replied Ted.

Hope had frozen and stopped stirring. It couldn't be. It simply couldn't be.

She slowly turned around.

To her horror it was.

Her stomach lurched. She knew not what caused it. Shock maybe?

Ted recovered first. "It's a pleasure to meet you Mrs. Walker, I hope it's not an inconvenience to have me for dinner?"

"I should think we would find you slightly too tough for our appetite," Hope replied.

Ted grinned. "Yes, I'm sure I would need days of marinating."

In those few seconds Hope recovered her composure. She put the spoon back in the pan, wiped her hands on her pinny, and then put out her hand towards Ted.

He took and shook it. His touch was soft and tender.

She snatched back her hand and put it behind her back. "Darling, why don't you two men wait in the living room and we'll set up the dining room and call you when it's ready."

"Righty-ho, come along Ted, let me show you my record collection, it's quite extensive."

"Are you alright dear?" Bessie asked when they left, for Hope had gone a little pale.

Hope smiled. "Yes, fine. I was just thrown by the unexpected company. In the whole year we've been married the only company we've had has been you and Douglas, it feels a bit strange that's all."

Bessie sensed there was more to it. "But a pleasant change?"

"Yes, of course. Now come on let's serve up this feast."

A little while later, the four of them were sitting around the dining table tucking into roast beef, roast potatoes, honey roasted parsnips and cabbage, and massive fluffy Yorkshire puddings.

"I think these are the best yorkies I've ever tasted," said Ted.

"The secret is to add a little baking powder, beat well and then leave it for an hour before cooking. They must go into an exceedingly hot tin of course, or they won't rise at all," Bessie explained.

Most of the meal was filled with pleasantries, but as time went by Hope's ire was building. She smiled and tried to squash the fact that she actually wanted to hit Ted over the head with a frying pan.

"And why hasn't a pleasant young man such as yourself got a sweetheart to go home to?" asked Bessie.

"Oh, yes, do tell," said Hope in a high-pitched voice which caused both Bessie and John to gape at her.

Ted lowered his knife and fork. "It's hard to find a girlfriend when you're an undertaker, it fair puts them off it do."

"Oh, that's a crying shame," said Bessie. "You're such a sweet young boy; I would have thought you'd have met your certain someone by now."

"I thought I'd found someone special once," he answered.

Hope threw him daggers, she literally wanted to lean across the table and strangle him. She was only slightly aware that her reaction was maybe slightly excessive.

"What happened?" asked John, totally unaware of his wife's crumbling composure.

"I met her at a dance. We had a super time, well I did. I know it sounds sissy-like, but I think I fell in love with her the moment I spotted her sitting on her own."

Hope had no control over the loud 'pff' that she uttered. John threw her a quick glance and she forced a weird looking smile onto her face. John's brows knitted together in bewilderment.

"Aww, what happened then? Did she not return your affection?" asked Bessie.

"You know, I'm sure that she did. It was funny, we seemed to have this instant connection."

"What went wrong then?" asked John before putting the last of his beef in his mouth.

"We made a date to meet the following Friday, outside the picture house."

"And she didn't show!" exclaimed Bessie.

Hope's second 'pff' was complete with a scowl that would send many a soldier running in the opposite direction.

"Actually, it was me who didn't show."

"Why ever not?" asked Hope sarcastically.

"My ma died."

There was complete silence for a full twenty seconds.

"Eee, lad I'm sorry to hear that."

Shivers ran down her spine, an imaginary dunking into a bath of icy water. It was hard to breathe. As clear as day, she could see that a year ago her life had reached a crossroads. She hadn't been able to see either path, and had blundered away blindly falling onto the path she was now on, one where she was married to John. What if?

What if?

What if?

"I remember when she died, Ted," said John. "Very sad day indeed. The way you looked after your three younger sisters did you credit, so it did."

He's not a cad, Hope thought. *He's a sincere young man*.

Everyone tried to be cheerful after that, but it wasn't possible. Shortly afterwards, Ted excused himself and set off for home.

"What a pleasant young man," said Bessie as they were clearing the table.

"Yes," agreed Hope, "a very pleasant young man."

Chapter 16

Monday, 12th October 1959

NOT LONG AFTER JOHN HAD LEFT FOR WORK, Hope put on her coat and hat and set off for the O'Brien & Son Undertaker's. She had to see Ted and apologize. Her step was brisk as she flew down the streets with haste.

A bell over the door tinkled as she went in. It wasn't even eight o'clock yet and she was relieved to find it open. It was a few moments before Ted appeared in the shop to see who had come in. He stopped short when he saw her.

"I waited over two hours for you, Ted."

"And I searched everywhere for you as soon as I could."

"I didn't know. I just assumed you didn't want to see me again."

"If that was the case I would have turned up to tell you so, I'm not the kind of man that would leave a lady standing around waiting."

"I'm sorry about your mother Ted, I truly am. And I'm sorry I didn't let you explain in the coffee house."

Ted was silent for a moment, his eyes firmly fixed on hers. "You've landed on your feet I see, it's funny I never took you for a gold-digger."

"Ted!"

"If you wouldn't mind leaving, we're not actually open yet. Please close the door behind you." He turned to walk back out of the shop and into the house.

"Ted how can you believe that of me? You're as bad as the old women from St Mary's judging me like that!"

He turned back to her, his face full of anger. "Well, let's examine the facts shall we? You'd only wanted to go on a date with me the week before you met John, oh yes I've done the maths! You only knew him a few weeks before you got married. He's old enough to be your father, and oh, he happens to be very comfortably provided for. What do you think it looks like Hope?"

"You don't know anything about me Ted O'Brien! If you did then you would know it doesn't matter what it *looks* like, what matters is the fact that John and I love each other."

She spun on her heels, marched out of the shop and slammed the door behind her.

"Grr!" Hope growled as she marched back home. "Men!"

"Women!" muttered Ted as he went back inside to help get his sisters ready for school.

"What's wrong with women?" asked Kay, his youngest sister.

"Everything," snapped Ted.

"Don't you like me, Ted?" she asked with big eyes.

He smiled at her and ruffled her hair. "Well, you're not a woman you're my sister, so I love you, silly."

173

"Ted, have you plant the new bulbs in the remembrance garden?" asked Bert, his father, coming into the shop.

"Done already Dad."

"Who was that in the shop?" asked Bert.

"Just a woman who'd lost her way."

"Did you set her straight?"

"I did indeed."

Wednesday, 14th October 1959

Hope had walked from the church to the undertakers shop three times and her feet were getting weary. She was just about to give up and head for home when she finally spotted Ted leaving the shop and heading down the road.

"Ted," she called out, and raced after him. He stopped and turned to watch her approach. For a moment they simply looked at each other. The 'what ifs' of life flashed through both their eyes.

"What can I do for you Hope?"

"I want to be friends, Ted. I understand now why you didn't turn up that day, and I'm sorry for the way I behaved at dinner on Sunday. Will you please forgive me? John really likes you, and well I do too, isn't life too short to spitting peas at each other?"

Ted grinned. "I haven't had a pea-shooter in years." He sucked in a ton of air, and then let it out slowly. "You're right of course, and I'm sorry if I judged you harshly."

"Thank you."

"You know I've never seen John so relaxed, so I have to admit you're good for him. He won't talk to anyone about it, but we know he never really got over Charlotte's…"

"Suicide. It's OK I know, John told me about it."

"He did? Well that's good."

"I've got to go Ted, but thanks, I'm glad we can be friends."

"Sure thing, see you around."

They parted ways. Hope was happy that they could be friends, but she also hoped they didn't run into each other too often, for there was a part of her heart she secretly knew would always belong to him.

Chapter 17

THE VERY WALLS SEEMED TO GROAN with the fact that she had picked up the stylus and put it back on the beginning of the record. Conway Twitty's *It's only Make Believe* filled the house… again.

Over and over she sang the words. Tears falling intermittently for the precise reason she knew not, just something inside her strangling her joy over her relationship with John.

"I won't have it," she screamed at the ceiling, before continuing with the song, "my only prayer will be, someday you'll care for me, but it's *only* make believe."

She loved John. There was no doubt of that inside her. Her life was perfect now they'd finally become husband and wife in the true sense of the union. He loved her, she knew he did. Maybe she resented his lingering love for Charlotte a little, but only a little, she did understand. Then again, it would have been more special to have a man who had given her his whole heart.

"Ack!" she moaned clasping her hands to her head. "I'm such an awful person. He loves me, it's enough."

She'd brought the single a few months ago. It had been released in May last year and she kept hearing it on the radio. The words had sunk into her spirit as her soul had been crying out to be loved by John. That was before the holiday. Now she had no idea why she kept playing it over and over. She felt like she was going nuts.

My one and only prayer

Is that someday you'll care

My hopes and my dreams come true

My one and only you

No-one will ever know

How much I love you so

Things were different now, he knew how much she loved him and she knew he loved her. Yet still the words pulled at her trying to drag her into the pits of despair. Why? Why?

She had to go out, she had to do something.

She switched off the record player, grabbed her coat and headed off down the street. She hadn't planned where she was going, but she found herself at the doors of the church.

Not sure if it would be open, she tried the handle. It opened. She stepped into the foyer and closed the door behind her. It was two o'clock in the afternoon and she wasn't sure if anyone would be inside, in fact she wasn't even sure she should be inside.

When she couldn't hear anything she stepped into the church and walked down to the first pew, where she sat down. Hope looked at the cross at the front of church.

"I guess I made a deal with you, didn't I," she said to the cross. "Well here I am. I don't really know what to do now, but I'm here."

"Here is a good place to start."

Hope startled and turned to see the vicar walking towards her.

Reverend Eamon O'Sullivan was the kind of man who could easily pretend to be Father Christmas. He was over six feet tall, had a mass of white gray curls on his head and sported a snow-white bushy beard and moustache. He just needed to switch his black cassock and white dog-collar for a red suit with a black belt. He was probably about sixty years old, but his cobalt-blue eyes shone with life.

"But where do I go from here?" Hope asked, generally lost.

"Come and have a cuppa with me," he said. "Everything always seems better with a pot of tea, don't you think?"

Hope looked unsure about following a strange man, albeit a holy one. He noticed her hesitation. "My wife's back at the vicarage, I'm sure she'd love to pop the kettle on for us."

Well that was different! Hope got up and followed Rev. O'Sullivan out of the church and down a short path, and into the vicarage. It was a huge house and Hope wondered how Mrs. O'Sullivan managed to keep it so lovely.

"You remember Mrs. Walker don't you Roisin?"

"Yes, of course I do. I don't think anyone will forget the surprise of the sudden marriage an' all."

Hope looked at her in surprise, but Roisin's eyes were sweet and kind and surrounded by laughter lines. Not a hint of malice was on her face.

"I'll make us some tea, why don't you go back to work dear?"

Eamon smiled. "Actually, that would be good, I've got that much to do it will keep me out of mischief for hours. You will stay and have tea with my wife won't you Hope?"

She could hardly say no. "Yes, of course."

With the vicar gone and the tea made the two ladies sat and stared at each other for a brief moment.

"Eamon is always bringing waifs and strays home, but you don't fit into that category, so I wonder what prompted him to bring you to me?"

Some people have an aura about them that makes you want to pour your heart out. Roisin was one of those people. She was a tiny woman, only five feet tall, her hair was a light brown totally flushed with gray. Her pale blue eyes were soft and un-judgmental. She was in fact the perfect vicar's wife.

"Why don't you tell me what's bothering you?"

Hope didn't hesitate, she poured out her grief, stopping only to blow her nose now and again, as she cried the entire time.

"What's wrong with me? Why am I not flooded with happiness now that John loves me so?"

179

"It seems to me like you have feelings for two men, and that is causing you great distress."

"I don't, I love John, I do, I do. He's everything I could want."

"He's also not your first love, and he's much older than you. Young people crave fun and excitement, while slightly older people yearn for nothing more than peace and quiet. It is just the way of the world."

"But I love being with John, we get along famously, I've never been happier."

At that Roisin couldn't help but laugh at the irony of a weeping girl declaring her happiness.

Lord, but Hope hated it when people laughed at her. She sat back in her chair and folded her arms.

"My sweet girl," said Roisin leaning across the table and patting Hope's arm. "It's no use carrying an umbrella if your shoes are leaking." She sat back and took a drink of tea.

"What does that mean?"

"I believe the hurts of your past are affecting the hopes of your future. Only by letting go of pain can we open up and allow hope to grow."

"I don't know how to do that."

"Ask ten people how to let go of the past, and you will receive ten different answers. Would you care to hear mine?"

Hope nodded.

"I was raised by an angry man. He swore by day and drank by night. Whenever I got in his way he beat me, I spent most of my childhood covered in bruises."

"I'm so sorry," said Hope, who would never have thought from looking at her that Roisin had anything but a great upbringing. She was so calm and full of peace.

"I left Galway when I was sixteen. I saved money for years and as soon as I could I got on a ferry and headed for England. I made my way to London seeking a better life. Instead, I found myself caught in the hands of wicked men who did wicked things."

Hope gasped, shocked.

"Eamon found me on the street one day. I had been in London for six months and I wanted to die. I thought my father was bad, but he was nothing compared to those men. Eamon took me to a safe house for women. In there I discovered I wasn't the only woman to suffer at the hands of wicked men. Some of them had been through things far worse than I. Eamon was always on the streets looking to rescue people, to lead them to the Lord. I had been brought up a Catholic but I had no belief in my heart. How could there be a God in a world of such suffering? It's not possible right?"

Hope couldn't answer, she was choked up.

"Eventually, I heard the Lord speak to me, not an audible voice you understand, but I received *knowledge*, an understanding, that can only be explained by belief. I decided to help the church help people after that. Eamon and I often worked together, and the rest is history as they say."

"My pain is nothing compared to yours," said Hope quietly.

"Don't you say that. Pain is pain. We each suffer in different ways, but there is no level of suffering in God's eyes, all pain is pain and He wishes to take it away from us."

Hope was crying. She wanted that. Not only to be pain-free but to believe, to have that *knowledge* that there was a Father in Heaven who cared for her, wanted her to be happy.

"I have something for you," said Roisin standing up, "won't be a minute." She left the room but came back quickly, holding a Bible in her hand. "Here, I would like you to have this."

"Oh, I can't," said Hope shaking her head.

"Please take it, you might not want to read it today or even tomorrow, but maybe one day you'll feel a pull to read and to learn more about God."

"Thank you," said Hope accepting the gift.

When she got home she placed the Bible in a drawer in the bedroom. She didn't know if she would ever want to read it, but somehow it gave her comfort to know she owned her own Bible.

Chapter 18

HOPE FELT BETTER AFTER TALKING to Roisin. She'd even taken the Bible out of the drawer a few times, flicking it open to different pages to see what it said. She didn't read much, but she did find herself reflecting on the words during the day.

Over the last few days she had done a great deal of soul searching. One day, out of the blue, she'd felt the urge to forgive her mother. This was a strange concept, a conundrum so to speak, for Agatha represented a figure that needed to be loved not forgiven. Agatha was her mother, parents did what they did, and she accepted that. To acknowledge she needed to forgive her was to admit that something had been done that wasn't right. And that's what she struggled with. Who was she to declare her mother's character was flawed? Wasn't Agatha simply a result of her own upbringing, which had been absent of affection? Who was Hope to judge?

But the desire to forgive, nay the need to forgive, wouldn't leave Hope in peace. One afternoon after all the cleaning and cooking had been done, she paced the living room floor.

Agatha hadn't beaten her children the way Roisin's father had beaten her. They'd received a smack around the head, an ear pulling, a lot of screaming maybe, but not an actual bashing. They might have been hungry some days, but they'd all survived and grown up relatively healthy. Like a raindrop slowly rolling down a leaf, the word 'neglect' landed in Hope's lap. She couldn't say unloved, because who knew but God what went on inside Agatha's head and heart, but neglect fitted like a hand in a glove.

As children they had laughed a lot, and they'd leaned on each other for love and support. It hadn't bothered her that she didn't have a father, or that her mother was opposed to shows of emotion and never hugged them.

Hope kept homing in on where she suddenly believed her issues lay. Neglect was one thing, abandonment another. Agatha had abandoned her children three times as Hope was growing up. Three times she ended up in an orphanage with her brother and sister. If she dared to lift off the scab of abandonment she realized that unloved was the word that lay under it.

Hope sobbed. Not from self-pity or anger, but from regret. "I forgive you, ma," she whispered and instantly received a measure of peace in her heart, the heart that had years ago been broken. Like putting pieces of a puzzle into place her heart was slowly mending, she just didn't know it yet.

Since Ted had come to dinner the thought of him had never left her. She'd been racked with guilt, how could she think of him when she was married to such a wonderful man? Now she realized her heart simply yearned to be loved. She was like a greedy child grabbing all the sweets

184

from a jar, or a dry sponge soaking up liquid after it's been placed in water. She craved love. She'd thought it had been security she'd always needed, now she knew she needed more than that.

And now she knew… she could let Ted go.

She didn't need the love of two men. John was more than enough.

Happiness slowly seeped back into her soul.

Maybe she was one of the luckiest people in the entire world; she was certainly going to do all that she could to make John happy. She would be a good wife, a better listener, a better cook …

Chapter 19

"A PARTY WILL BE FUN," argued John. "Come on let's go. The O'Brien's have been good to me ever since…"

"It's alright John, you can say her name, ever since Charlotte died."

"Yes, they were awfully supportive back then."

"Then how can we refuse?"

"Thank you darling. We needn't stay long if you don't want, but it will be good to go. They've invited Bessie too, so you'll have someone to talk to besides my lovely self!"

Hope playfully slapped his arm with the tea-towel.

"Does she know yet?"

"No, I thought I'd tell you first, and then I was going to go round."

"I'll go," said Hope taking off her coverall apron. "I can have a chat with her about what we can take with us."

"It's Emma's eighteenth you say?"

"Yes. They're having family and a few friends over. They said there's no need to buy a present."

"Stuff-and-nonsense! Of course we've to get a present."

***

"Do say you'll come, Bessie, I should be lost without you."

"I don't think my old bones can handle a party. Eighteen you say? Why that will be too boisterous for me."

"I'm sure it won't, and if it is we will all come home as soon as you want."

Hope's face was a picture of pleading, and Bessie relented. "Oh, fine, but if they play loud music I shall be on my way home with a quick march."

"Don't you want to go to the party yourself, Hope?"

"I didn't get very enthusiastic when John first told me, I must confess. But John wants to go, and so now I do!"

Hope was being cheery but Bessie detected a touch of resistance. "Is it Ted you don't want to see?"

"No, it's nothing like that."

"Umm, well you were a little off when he came around here for dinner a couple of weeks ago."

"I don't have anything against him, Bessie, honest." With that Hope leant over and gave Bessie a kiss on the cheek and a big hug. "Now what shall we bake to take with us?"

Saturday, 7th October 1959

Hope had found something she had seen other young ladies buying and she was sure Emma would like it. It was a necklace and earing set, two strings of faux turquoise and coral stones and two pairs of stud earrings, one in turquoise and one in coral so Emma could pick and mix depending on her outfit. The set came in a box and Hope had wrapped it in colored paper and tied it with some ribbon.

Bessie and Hope had cooked some flapjacks, which they thought would be suitable for the children and wouldn't break too many young teeth, and two huge apple pies.

At six-thirty they put on their winter coats, for it was blowing a gale, and with gifts, pies and a bottle of wine they climbed into a taxi (John had insisted on ordering one because of the cold and because Bessie was with them) and they set off for the O'Brien's home.

There was a sign on the funeral shop window that said *'party started just come on in'* so they opened the door and went in. The bell tinkled and before they had taken two steps a young girl came running in.

She looked about ten, a pretty little thing with black curly hair. "Come on," she called, "we've started already."

With smiles at each other they followed their little host.

The funeral parlor had been given a makeover. Chairs lined the walls instead of being in rows, and the area where a coffin was normally displayed now hosted a long table laden with delectable food. Balloons hung from the ceiling and a small table sat in the corner covered in birthday presents.

"You put your name on that?" The little girl asked with a nod towards the gift Hope carried.

"We have indeed," replied Hope.

"Then I'll put it on the table for you. Pa said to be sure there was a name on everything so that Emma can write 'er thank-you letters."

Hope smiled and passed it over.

"Thanks for coming, John."

"It's a pleasure Bert," answered John while shaking hands with Ted's father.

"And you know Hope and Bessie already," John stated.

Bert shook hands with each of the ladies, "So glad you could make it."

"Pa, Pa, uncle Wilfred's arrived," said the young host tugging on Bert's jacket.

"Please, make yourself at home and get a drink, I'll be back for a chat later," said Bert.

The three moved over to the food table and added their pies and flapjacks to it, before moving over to another table which hosted a good supply of drinks.

"Let me pour you all a drink," said Ted appearing out of nowhere.

"Hi Ted, quite a bash you've got going on here for your Emma," said Bessie.

"Well you're only eighteen once, I don't think she's staying long. She wants to say her 'ello's to everyone and share some scran, and then her friends are coming to take her dancing."

"How marvelous," said Bessie.

"And which of your sisters is the sweet little thing that greeted us on arrival?" asked Hope. She was slightly wary, not sure how Ted would respond to her presence.

Ted grinned. "That'll be our Kay, you'd think this was her party, she's that excited!"

"She's very pretty," said Hope.

Ted looked at her straight on for the first time since appearing, and smiled. "Please don't tell her that, we don't want her getting any funny ideas in that head of hers."

"Mum's the word," said Hope putting a finger on her lips.

Once they all had drinks in hand they moved across the room where they spotted an empty chair that Bessie could sit on.

Music was being played on a record player in the corner of the room; the atmosphere was jolly and quite loud.

Ted stayed with them and the four of them were having a general conversation when all of the sudden a loud burst of laughter came from their left.

They turned around and saw a group of people gathered around an elderly lady who was sitting in a chair holding court.

"Let me introduce you to my aunty Margaret," said Ted, nodding towards the sprightly woman in the chair.

They followed Ted across the room to where the woman sat in a high-backed chair.

"Queenie," said Ted, his voice slightly raised. "These are my friends Hope, John and Bessie. I've brought them over to say 'ello to you."

"Who?"

"My friends, Hope, John and Bessie," he said leaning in towards her right ear.

"Ooh 'ello Hope, that's a lovely name you have, so it is," said the old woman.

"Speak on her right side, she hears much better with that ear."

"Yes please son, I'll have another beer if you'd fetch me one."

Ted winked at Hope, and mouthed, "I won't be long."

"Well now, aren't you a fine gen-tell-man," Margaret said holding out her vein-covered hand to John.

Always the gentleman, he took her hand and bought it to his lips and placed a light kiss over her crinkled hand.

"You're not a bad looking man," said Margaret winking at Hope.

"Why thank you," said John.

"You don't seem very old, your voice sounds older, but your face has fared well, young it is. How old are you?"

"I'm forty-three," said John grinning.

"Oh, I wouldn't have put you at that age."

"Why thank you." He beamed.

"I would have put you firmly approaching sixty."

Hope choked on her drink, and had to stand back a bit to hide her laughter.

Ted reappeared with a shandy. "Don't mind Queenie, she's not had new glasses for over thirty years. No amount of telling her she needs new ones will convince her."

"Now, I never asked you to dilute my beer with lemonade did I?" she moaned at Ted.

"It's refreshing aunty."

She took a sip and scowled at him, but quickly followed it with a big glug.

"Young man, where's your manners? Now go and fetch the lady here a chair so she can sit next to me," said Margaret.

Ted was straight back with a chair for Bessie. "Thank you," said Bessie, "my legs were beginning to grumble I have to say."

Margaret tapped her arm with a knowing nod. "Got to milk our age," she said with an exaggerated wink. "What else is old age good for but to make the youngsters run around after us? That's an awfully pretty cardigan you've got on there, Bessie, did you knit it yourself?"

Bessie beamed at the compliment. "I did indeed. I love to knit; it's how I spend my evenings. I normally make the grandchildren things and parcel them up and post them to London. But I thought a couple of months back that I could do with a new cardigan, so here it is."

"It's beautiful," agreed Hope, sitting herself down on the arm of Bessie's big chair.

"I bought the pattern in Woolworths, but it's a Lion Brand and says on the back it's from America. I picked it because I like the collar and the pockets, come in very handy they do."

"Me aunty once sent me a fur coat from America, so she did," said Margaret.

"A fur coat?" asked Bessie, "you must have looked extremely grand in that."

"Well, I used to wear it to Mass every Sunday, so I did, and I had every clown in the village looking at me."

"You must have looked lovely in it then," said Hope.

"Oh no, it wasn't that, that kept them looking."

"You must have had a very wealthy aunt," said John.

"Not really, the coat was full of holes you see, goodness knows where she got it from. I only wore it because it was the only coat that was all mine!"

"Aye, back in the day we had to make do, didn't we," said Bessie.

"Sure did. It was 'orrible that coat, but kept me warm so I'll not complain. Not like the youngsters these days, they've always got something to complain about," added Margaret. "The only thing I get in the post these days are bills. No more parcels from America, now that's something I'll not complain about. The bills though, I don't know what's happening to the world with the prices of everything, tis a disgrace it is."

"Things are hard since the war," chipped in John.

"We all thought things would go back to normal when rationing stopped, but it never happened. Don't think I can remember what normal is anymore," said Bessie.

"Did you lose your good man in the war, Bessie?" asked Margaret.

"Aye, I did. And you?"

"Aye, sad days, sad days," said Margaret. "My neighbor Henry came back from the war he did, he was one of the lucky ones. But he's got awful sad these days, so he has."

"Why's that?" asked Hope.

"Well, his Frieda died you see."

"Oh I'm sorry, was that his wife?" asked Hope.

"No, his chicken."

"His chicken?" Hope tried not to laugh as she asked, "what did Frieda die of then?"

"Well it wouldn't lay anymore would it."

"Lay?" asked John.

"Eggs, she stopped laying eggs so it was the death of her."

"Poor thing," said Bessie.

"My brother's a rum-un yer know," said Margaret getting serious and sitting up straight in her seat.

"Why's that?" asked John.

"He's always up to shenanigans he is, like last week with the monkeys."

"What happened?" asked Hope.

"Well, he says he was going about his business when some Englishman asked him if he would take fifteen monkeys over to Chester Zoo for him, and for his troubles he'd pay him ten pounds. Well, Patrick has a truck, so he agreed. A few hours later the Englishman spotted our Patrick coming back into town, with the monkeys still in the back of the truck. So he waved him down and demanded to know what was going on. Well... said Patrick, we had a good time at the zoo, and as I've still got some change from the ten pounds I thought I would take them for an ice cream."

There was ten seconds of absolute silence before the room around them erupted into laughter.

"You blooming Englishmen all think we Paddies is stupid, but we always get the last laugh."

"So we do Margaret, so we do. Now stop teasing the poor man and let's have some scran," said Ted.

The rest of the evening continued to be lots of fun, especially when Bert's brothers started playing the fiddle and the majority of the room joined in singing Irish ditties.

They were still laughing after they had dropped off Bessie and arrived home.

"Shall we have a drink before retiring?" John asked.

"You grab a whiskey John, I'm parched, I'm going to get a glass of water."

As she filled her glass from the tap, music coming from the living room made her smile, John had put Dean Martin on, *Everybody Loves Somebody* floated in the air and made her feel like dancing. As she walked into the living room she kicked off her shoes and swung her hips as she approached John.

He took the glass off her and put it on the table.

He reached out and grabbing her hand, swung her under his arm and pulled her close to his chest. Instantly, his arm was around her waist and he started dancing her around the sofa.

She laid her head on his chest and sighed. This was love, this wanting to be touched… to be close… to make each other happy.

After dancing to *Volare*, Hope asked John to move the needle to *Sway*.

As John waltzed her around the furniture she felt her heart would burst with happiness.

Sometime later, they lay in bed together facing each other.

John reached over and gently moved Hope's hair off her face. "You're my beautiful little chatter-box."

"And you, Mr. Walker are my prince on a white horse, and I thank God for you."

He leaned up on his elbow and moved to within an inch of her face. "That's the loveliest thing you could say to me," he whispered before closing in and kissing her.

Chapter 20

Wednesday, 25th November 1959

"JOHN, JOHN... CAN YOU HEAR ME?" Hope shifted from one foot to the other as she stood inside the red telephone box at the end of the street.

"Yes, I'm here, no need to shout. What's wrong, what's happened?"

For a moment Hope was silent, savoring the moment. "I know I should wait until you come home, but well, you know how impatient I am. I'm just bursting to tell you, I couldn't wait another moment. It's alright isn't it? I mean you won't get in trouble at work for accepting my telephone call?"

"It's fine Hope, but for goodness sake do tell me what's wrong."

"Wrong? Oh there's nothing wrong. No I'd never call you at work to give you bad news, you silly thing, that would be far too distressing for you."

"Hope, I'm finding this telephone call mighty distressing at the moment, will you please tell me what's happened?"

"Well a few weeks ago I noticed I felt slightly odd, but I wasn't sure what it was. And well, I mentioned this to Bessie the other day because I keep getting these funny turns, and well... she said that I should pop along to the doc's post-haste and let him check me out."

"My God Hope, are you telling me you're ill?"

"Now who's impatient? So, I went to see him last week, and he sent me to the nurse to run some tests and I've been back to see him just now for the results."

"Woman! You'll be the death of me! What's wrong?"

"We're having a baby, John."

There was complete silence on the line. She waited a moment and then shouted as she held the bottom half of the phone in front of her mouth. "I said we're having a baby, John, did you hear me?"

There were a few seconds of silence before John blurted out, "Woman you're going to make me deaf, I've said there's no need to shout." But as he was speaking there was a chorus of shouts and yells going on behind him.

Hope heard someone yell, "Old Walker's going to be a father!" which was followed by a bellow of men shouting out their congratulations.

"You see," said John eventually, "the whole office heard you!"

Hope got the giggles.

"How do you feel? Are you well? Is everything going to be alright?"

She heard the panic in his voice and knew he was thinking of Charlotte's miscarriages. "Yes John, I'm fine, extremely robust and healthy the doctor called me."

John sighed. "Oh my darling, you have made me the happiest man alive. I'm going to finish work now and come home early so I can take care of you."

Hope laughed. "Don't be silly, I'm fine I don't need looking after. I'll see you at tea time."

"OK, see you later, and Hope…"

"Yes?"

"I love you to the moon and back."

"I love you too."

***

Despite her urging him to stay at work, John couldn't contain his excitement and went to speak to his manager about taking a half day's holiday.

Knowing John for a long time and knowing his history with Charlotte, his boss said, "John, take the afternoon on us, this is a momentous day."

With thanks to his manager, and waves to his work colleagues, John grabbed his hat and coat and went running out of the building, taking the steps two at a time.

Lime Street train station was quieter than normal because it was lunch time. John thought how pleasant it would be if he could travel to and from work every day with only this number of people around.

In the station foyer was a stand selling flowers. He picked up a bunch of Roses and was about to pay for them when he had a change of mind. "Let's take a mixture," he said to the seller, and began picking up bunches of mauve

Sweet Peas and purple Verbena just as his glance fell upon sunflowers.

"Perfect!" In the end he purchased six different bunches of flowers, a beautiful gift for his beautiful wife. He paid for the flowers and raced out of the Renaissance Revival styled building. He took the steps outside the station two at a time, his heart singing, his joy complete.

He never saw the red Alfa Romeo. He didn't hear the screeching of tires. Didn't feel the impact as his body hit the bonnet and went flying over the car. One second he was there, and the next he wasn't.

"John."

He turned towards the voice and happiness sprang in his heart. "Charlotte." She came from nowhere but was suddenly in his arms. He held her tight and covered her head with kisses. "Oh, my love, I've missed you."

After a moment she pulled away from him. Smiling gently up at him, she took hold of his hand. "It's time to go John."

"Go? Go where?"

And then he noticed.

His body lying on the road.

Blood pouring from his head.

People rushing from all corners to come and see if there was anything they could do for the man who hadn't stopped to look but who had raced straight into the road.

Scattered all around him – like fragments of beauty upon a scene of tragic proportions – lay an array of colorful flowers.

Upon his chest lay a single bright yellow sunflower.

"I can't leave her!"

Charlotte squeezed his hand. "You have to my love."

"But she's going to have a baby."

"I know. Come now, we need to go home."

"I can't leave her on her own, Charlotte, I just can't do that to her, she's been through so much in her short life."

"I promise everything is going to be OK."

And in that second he suddenly 'knew' she was right, for the verse long ago written, spoken often in church and seldom believed, bloomed in his spirit as truth. *And we know that in all things God works for the good of those who love him, who have been called according to His purpose. (Romans 8:28)*

"And I do love Him," said John.

"And He loves you, John. Now come, it is time for us to go home."

And so John left this world of pain and sorrow, and walked into the Light of a new life, with his first true love beside him.

Chapter 21

Sunday, 26th April 1960

JOHN HAD BEEN GONE FOR FIVE MONTHS NOW. It had been so painful that Bessie had worried Hope would miscarry. But Hope was determined to have this child; this little piece inside her was all that was left of her special man. John would live on through this child, and she had been on her knees many times praying for God's blessing.

It seemed such a pity that true belief had come to her only after her husband's death. It would have pleased him no end, she was sure, to know that she now had faith and loved reading the Bible as well.

She wasn't sure she would have coped without Bessie, the woman, despite her age and fragility, had turned into a powerhouse of comfort and advice. The baby kicked inside her, causing her to smile.

"Hello little one," she said rubbing her tummy. "Mummy loves you. I'll always love you and take care of you." She had to love this child to bits, for she had to love her (for Hope was convinced it was a girl) enough for both parents.

"Kicking?" asked Bessie coming to sit next to her at the kitchen table.

Hope smiled and nodded.

"And how's *he* getting on," Bessie asked nodding her head in the direction of the stairs. At that precise moment something was dropped on the floor and the visitor could be heard cursing quietly.

"He's patient," replied Hope.

"Umm, so he should be too. Be indecent for him to be courting you so soon after you've buried your husband."

Just then they heard him coming down the stairs.

"Dinner's ready, you're just in time to help me dish up," said Bessie without looking up.

"I'll wash my hands," said Ted, going towards the sink.

"Don't let her boss you around too much," said Hope.

"Oh, its fine, with three sisters I'm well used to it."

"Did you manage to build it OK?"

Ted twisted by the sink so he could look at her. "It's all ready for the little 'un."

"I'll be back shortly," said Hope, getting up and waddling over to the stairs.

"I'll come with you," said Ted drying his hands.

"Oh, no you don't young man; you can fetch that there chicken out of the oven for me." Bessie clamped her hand onto his arm. "Leave her a bit," she whispered to him.

Upstairs Hope went into her old bedroom that had been decorated as a nursery. Ted had just put the cot together, and Hope went over to look at it.

"I'll take good care of your child, John," she whispered. "We'll never forget you." She was amazed how easily the tears fell. She had accepted John's accident, but it still felt as raw and as painful as it did the day the policemen had knocked on her door with the news. She blamed herself, if she hadn't called him, he wouldn't have been rushing home. It was all her fault. He'd even told her that she would be the death of him. Bessie scolded her, and the vicar contradicted her, but she felt it in her bones, it was all her fault. She hadn't been good enough to have a man like John love her. She didn't deserve Ted's affection either, but she was thankful for it.

He'd spoken plain and straight when he'd come to see her a month after the funeral. 'I'll wait until the cows come home,' he'd told her. 'But I ain't going anywhere, and one day I hope you will love me as I love you.'

Tears poured. "Oh God, how do I deserve the love of two good men?"

And as clear as day, Hope heard God speak to her for the first time.

For I know the plans I have for you, plans to prosper you and not to harm you, plans to give you a hope and a future. (Jeremiah 29:11)

The knowledge of God's unending love and patience filled the nursery with light and warmth. Hope sank to her knees in awe. Who was she that God should speak to her? How could she be deserving of such compassion? She didn't know the answers, but one thought rang through her soul bringing an abundant overflowing of joy – it would be her hope and not her hurts that would guide her from this day forth.

She radiated gratitude in full bloom, like the sunflower, with its deep color and soft petals bursting with a promise of harvest. For you see she finally had the answer to the question that had tormented her for so long… Yes, broken people can be made whole again. With hope, love and time the deepest wounds can be mended. It didn't mean that the rubbish things would cease to happen, but she now knew that *hope* would carry her through. The pain of rejection, and the loss of John would never be forgotten, but the gift God had given her of a new life growing within her would be a balm with healing properties. When the time was right, she would open the romantic doors of her heart once more, and allow herself to return Ted's love.

For where there is *hope* there is the promise of a better life.

Hope…
Is being able to see that there is light, despite
all the darkness.
Desmond Tutu

Thank you so much for reading

If you enjoyed Hope's story could I please encourage you to leave me a review? Without reviews a book never succeeds and I would really appreciate your endorsement and support. Many thanks.

1958 ~ Liverpool

Mum working at a garage

Lady on the left is my nan, this is her second wedding day, my mum is far right, aged 18

MORE IN THIS SERIES

If you'd like to know more about my books please check out my web.

http://www.tntraynor.uk

You can also find me on Facebook.

https://www.facebook.com/groups/292316321513651

Or Twitter: @tracy_traynor

If you enjoyed this book you might also enjoy one of my other books in this series.

MULTI AWARD WINNING SERIES

WOMEN OF COURAGE

Inspired by the life of Moira Smith 1912 - 1985	Inspired by the Welsh Revival 1904 - 1905	A 2020 Love Story	A story of hope 1958	
				Standalone Stories with a theme of courage and love

Coming in 2022

The last book in the Women of Courage Series

Set in 1661, Brianna's faith is such that when she prays for people they are healed. Stories about her miraculous healings put her under the eye of The Witch Hunter General, and a chase across England begins.

If you would like to receive updates by receiving my email newsletter, please sign up at https://sendfox.com/tntraynor

In my newsletter will be updates about my books, book competitions, a book review from me and ebooks that are on offer or free by other authors. The newsletter is only quarterly, so only 4 a year ☺ no spam or sharing of details.

Thank you for reading, I value your support, for without readers there would be no point in writing – and I do so love to write!

Lots of blessings to you,

Tracy

Printed in Great Britain
by Amazon

12285675R00119